What do you think about in the seconds before death?

Have you ever considered that? You're probably considering it right now.

In Mack's case he was thinking about his life. Which, prior to Grimluk suddenly informing him of his importance in an age-old struggle between good and evil, had been pretty boring.

And Mack was thinking about how great boring is. Boring is excellent, compared to dying.

In those last seconds he was thinking about his mom. And screaming. And his dad. And screaming.

And he was feeling guilty because now the world would not be saved and the Pale Queen would enslave all of humanity. She would probably outlaw video games and movies and fro-yo and Toaster Strudel and all the truly good things in the world.

And then there was the screaming.

And suddenly Mack heard a voice, audible even over the shriek of the wind whipping past.

He didn't think he recognized the voice. Then again, it's sometimes hard to recognize voices when you're screaming and hurtling to your death.

"Halk-ma simu (ch)ias!"

Praise for
The Magnificent 12: The Call

"A terrific start, with an elaborate website festooned with games and contests to ease the wait for sequels."
—ALA *Booklist* (starred review)

"The story's abundant action and humor should win over readers." —*Publishers Weekly*

"Sure to win many fans and fly off the shelves."
—*Kirkus Reviews* (starred review)

"Welcome to Monty Python meets *The Lord of the Rings*. The future of all civilization rests in the hands of a middle school wimp with more phobias than muscle groups, and saving the world has never been funnier."
—Gordon Korman, author of *Pop*, *Zoobreak*, and two books in the 39 Clues series

"A thrill ride through time with cool monsters, relatable heroes, *and* big laughs. What more could a kid ask for?"
—Patrick Carman, author of *The Land of Elyon*, *Atherton*, and *Skelton Creek*

"Fantastically funny and fast-paced, *The Magnificent 12* is written with a dry wit and a wonderful economy of words." —Angie Sage, author of the Septimus Heap series

Also by Michael Grant

Gone
Hunger
Lies
Plague
Fear
Light
The Magnificent 12: The Call
The Magnificent 12: The Trap

MICHAEL GRANT

THE MAGNIFICENT 12

BOOK THREE

THE KEY

KATHERINE TEGEN BOOKS
An Imprint of HarperCollins Publishers

Katherine Tegen Books is an imprint of HarperCollins Publishers.

The Magnificent 12: The Key

www.harpercollinschildrens.com

Library of Congress Cataloging-in-Publication Data
Grant, Michael.
    The key / Michael Grant. — 1st ed.
        p.   cm. — (The Magnificent 12 ; [3])
    Summary: Twelve-year-old Mack MacAvoy and a team of other twelve-year-
olds travel to Europe to find a special Key that will help them defeat the Pale
Queen and save the world from destruction.
    ISBN 978-0-06-183371-7
    [1. Fantasy.   2. Adventure and adventurers—Fiction.   3. Good and evil—
Fiction.   4. Humorous stories.]   I. Title.
PZ7.G7671Key   2012   2012012715
[Fic]—dc23   CIP
                                                                 AC

Typography by Amy Ryan
13 14 15 16 17   OPM   10 9 8 7 6 5 4 3 2 1
❖
First paperback edition, 2013

The author wishes to acknowledge the usefulness of www.scotranslate.com in rendering decent,
proper English into a version of Scots.

For Katherine, Jake, and Julia

BOOK THREE

THE KEY

One

"Let me out of here, you crazy old man!" Mack cried.

"Ye'll ne'er lea' 'ere alive. Or at least ye wilnae be alive fur lang. Ha-ha-ha!" Which was Scottish, more or less, for, "You'll never leave here alive. Or at least you won't be alive for long. Ha-ha-ha!"

The Scots are known for butchering the English language and for their ingenuity with building things. The first steam engine? Scottish guy invented it. The first raincoat? A Scot invented that, too. The first television, telephone, bicycle—all invented by Scots.

They're a very handy race.

And the first catapult designed to hurl a twelve-year-old boy from the top of the tallest tower in a castle notable for its tall towers? It turns out that, too, was invented by a Scot, and his name was William Blisterthöng MacGuffin.

The twelve-year-old boy in question was David MacAvoy. All his friends called him Mack, and so did William Blisterthöng MacGuffin, although they were definitely not friends.

"Ye see, Mack, mah wee jimmy, whin ah cut th' rope, they stones thare, whit we ca' th' counterweight, drop 'n' yank this end doon while at th' same time ye gang flying thro' th' air."

Mack did see this.

Actually the catapult was surprisingly easy to understand, although Mack had never been good at science. The catapult was shaped a little like a long-handled spoon that balanced on a backyard swing set. A rough-timbered basket full of massive granite rocks was attached to the short handle end of the spoon. The business end of the spoon, where it might have contained chicken noodle soup or minestrone, was filled with Mack.

Mack was tied up. He was a hog-tied little bundle of fear.

The spoon, er, catapult, had been cranked so that the rock end was in the air and the Mack end was down low. A rope held the Mack end down—a rope that twanged with the effort of holding all that weight in check. A rope whose short fibers were already popping out. A rope that looked rather old and frayed to begin with.

William Blisterthöng MacGuffin, a huge, burly, red-haired, red-bearded, red-eyebrowed, red-chest-haired, red-wrist-haired man in a plaid skirt[1] held a broadsword that could, with a single sweeping motion, cut the rope. Which would allow the rocks to swiftly drag down the short end of the spoon while hurling Mack through the air.

"Ye invaded mah privacy uninvited, ye annoying besom. And now ye've drawn the yak o' th' Pale Queen, ye gowk!"

Or in decent, proper English, "You invaded my privacy uninvited, you annoying brat. And now you've drawn the eye of the Pale Queen, you ninny."

---

1 Okay, call it a kilt if you want; it still looks like a skirt.

How far could the catapult throw Mack? Well, a well-made catapult . . . actually, you know what? This particular kind of catapult is called a trebuchet. *Treh-boo-shay*. Let's use the proper vocabulary out of respect for Mack's imminent death.

A well-made trebuchet (this one looked pretty well made) can easily hurl 100 kilos (or approximately two Macks) a distance of 1,000 feet.

Let's picture 1,000 feet, shall we? It's three football fields. It's just a little less than if you laid the Empire State Building down flat. It's long enough that if you started screaming at the moment of launch, you'd have time to scream yourself out, take a deep breath, check your messages, and scream yourself out again.

That would be pretty bad.

Unfortunately it got worse. The castle tower was about 300 feet tall. The castle itself sat perched precariously atop a spur of lichen-crusted rock that shot 400 feet above the surrounding land.

So let's do the math. Three hundred feet plus 400 feet makes a 700-foot vertical drop. And the horizontal distance was about 1,000 feet.

At the end of all that math was a second ruined castle, which sat beside Loch Ness.

In Loch Ness was the Loch Ness monster. But Mack wouldn't be hitting the lake; he'd be hitting the stone walls of that second castle, Urquhart Castle. He would hit it so hard, his body would become part of the mortar between the stones of that castle.

"Dae ye huv ony lest words tae say afore ah murdurr ye?"

"Yes! I have last words to say before you murder me! Yes! My last words are: don't murder me!"

Mack could have used some magical words of Vargran. He was totally capable of speaking it. Totally.

If.

If Mack had taken some time to study what words of Vargran had been given to him and his friends. Sadly, when Mack might have been studying he rode the London Eye Ferris wheel instead. And the next time he could have been studying he downloaded a game on his phone instead and played Mage Gauntlet for six hours. And the next time . . . Well, you get the idea.[2]

So instead of whipping out some well-chosen magical words, Mack could only say, "Seriously:

2 The moral of that story is: it's fun to play games on your phone! Wait, that can't be right.

please don't murder me."

Which is just pathetic.

Look, we all know Mack is the hero of the story. And we all know the hero can't be killed. So there's no way he's just going to be slammed into a ruined castle and—

"Cheerio the nou, ye scunner," MacGuffin said, and he swung the sword.

The blade parted the frayed rope.

But wait, seriously? Mack's going to die?

Gravity worked the way it usually does, and the big basket of rocks dropped like a big basket of rocks.

Hey! If Mack dies, the world is doomed and the Pale Queen wins!

"Aaaahhh!" Mack screamed.

He flew like a cannonball toward certain death.

Let's avert our gazes from the place and moment of impact.

No one wants to see what happens to a kid when he hits a stone wall—it's just too gruesome and disturbing. So let's back the story up a little and see how Mack got himself into this mess to begin with.

In fact, let's do some ellipses to signal that we are

going back in time . . . to the day before . . .

Before . . .

"Ahhhhh!" Mack cried, gripping the dashboard. He was seated next to Stefan, who was driving.

"Aieeee!" Xiao cried, gripping the back of Mack's seat.

"Acchhh!" Dietmar cried, hugging himself and rocking back and forth.

"Yeee hah!" Jarrah shouted, flashing a huge grin as she pumped her fist in the seat behind Stefan.

A car—it happened to be yellow—roared straight for them, horn blaring, headlights flashing, driver forming his mouth into a terrified O shape.

Stefan jerked the wheel left and stomped on the gas. This was accidental. He had meant to stomp on the brakes but he was confused. He didn't really know how to drive.

"Other way, other way, otherwayotherwayother-way—aaaaaaaahhhh!" Mack yelled as Stefan drove the rented car into a traffic circle.

Now, in most of the world the cars in a traffic circle go counterclockwise. The exceptions are England, Wales, Australia, New Zealand, Japan, a few other countries, and Scotland.

This happened to be a Scottish traffic circle.

Those of you who've read the first two books about the Magnificent Twelve may recall that our hero, Mack MacAvoy, was twelve years old. In fact, being twelve was an important part of being a member of the Magnificent Twelve. Because it wasn't just any random twelve people. It was twelve twelve-year-olds, each of whom possessed the *enlightened puissance*.

And remembering that, you might also be thinking, Who rents a car to a twelve-year-old?

Well, perhaps you're forgetting that Stefan was fifteen—although he was in the same grade as Mack. Stefan, not being one of the Magnificent Twelve, but more of a bodyguard, could have been any age. He happened to be fifteen, and he looked eighteen. Which is still not old enough to be renting a car. Especially when you don't have a driver's license.

But you may also remember the part about Mack being given a million-dollar credit card.

Cost of car rental: 229.64 GBP.[3]

Cost of the gift certificate to Jenners department

---

3 GBP means Great British Pounds. It's like money, but with pictures of the queen.

store in Edinburgh in the name of the car-rental clerk: 3,000.00 GBP.

Yeah: it's amazing what you can do with a million dollars. Renting a car is the least of it.

"There's a truck!" Mack shouted.

"It's called a lorry here!" Dietmar yelled in his know-it-all way.

"I don't care if it's called a—"

"Jog a little to the right there," Jarrah suggested quite calmly, and put her hand on Stefan's powerful shoulder. Stefan did as he was told.

The truck or lorry or whatever it was called let go a horn blast that could have shattered a plate glass window and went shooting past so close that, *bang*, it knocked the left side mirror off the little red car.

"The mirror!" Xiao cried.

"Enh," Stefan said, and shrugged. "I wasn't using it anyway."

He wasn't. As far as Mack could tell, Stefan wasn't even using the windows, let alone the mirrors, and was more or less driving according to some suicidal instinct.

The car had seemed like a bad idea from the start,

but Mack didn't like to come across all bossy, or like he was a wimp or something. One of the problems with having twenty-one identified phobias—irrational fears—is that people tend to think you're a coward. Mack was not a coward: he just had phobias. Which meant there were twenty-one things he was cowardly about—tight spaces, sharks, needles, oceans, beards, and a few others—but he was brave enough about most things.

So when it had been pointed out to him that having made it by train from London to Edinburgh, Scotland, the best way to get from there to Loch Ness was by car, he'd gone along. To demonstrate that he was not a huge wimp.

How was that going? Like this:

"Gaaa-aah-ahh!" Dietmar commented.

BAM!

Rattle rattle rattle rattle.

Thump!

The car hit the low curb guarding the center of the circle, bounced over the lumpy grass, swerved around some sort of monument, narrowly missed a pair of Mini Coopers—one red, one tan—and bounced out of the other side of the circle and onto the main road.

Mack, Xiao, and Dietmar all took the first breath they'd inhaled in several minutes.

Stefan said, "Is there a drive-through in this country? I'm starving."

And Jarrah said, "I'm so hungry I could eat a horse and chase the jockey."

Jarrah and Stefan: obviously they were not quite normal.

Having survived the traffic circle, the gang found a gas station that also had food. They bought prepackaged sandwiches and sodas. They topped the car off with gas. And that's when Mack noticed a van he had noticed earlier. There was nothing remarkable about the van—it was beige, which is the world's least noticeable color. But Mack was a kid who noticed things and he noticed that this van had a dent on one side. A small thing. But what were the odds that there were two tan vans with the same dent?

He had first noticed this van way back just outside Edinburgh, and now that Mack looked closer, it seemed the windshield was tinted. Which would be a perfectly normal thing where Mack was from—the

Arizona desert, where the sun shone 360 out of 365 days—but was pretty strange here in Scotland, where the sun shone 5 days out of 365.

"That van has been following us," Mack said as the five of them leaned against their car eating.

No one questioned him. They'd all learned that when Mack noticed something, he noticed it right.

So they leaned there and watched the van. Which maybe was watching them back.

"I'll go ask them what's up," Stefan said.

"No," Mack said, shaking his head. "Maybe it's a coincidence. Maybe they're just going to the same place we are."

"That is perhaps likely," Dietmar said. "Loch Ness is very famous, and people will be coming from all over to see it."

Dietmar spoke flawless English but his accent was strange at times, and Mack had to struggle to resist mocking him. As leader of the group, Mack had to behave in a very mature way. Mostly he did. But in his mind he was saying, "Zat iss peerheps likely," in a snooty voice.

He didn't dislike Dietmar; Dietmar was fine. But

it wasn't possible to like everyone equally. Dietmar was very smart and made sure everyone knew it. And he was better-looking than Mack—at least Mack thought so, since Dietmar had perfectly straight blond hair while Mack had boring curly brown hair. As a result of that, Mack was pretty sure Xiao thought Dietmar was fascinating.

Mack, however, found Xiao fascinating. So he didn't really want her to find Dietmar more fascinating than him. Mack wasn't exactly sure why he found Xiao so interesting. A year ago he would have barely noticed her if he'd met her. But lately he had looked with slightly more interest at girls. It wasn't a really focused attention just yet. But it was attention.

Possibly it was because he had seen Xiao in her true form. She was, after all, a dragon. Not a fire-breathing, leathery-winged type, but the less terrifying and more spiritual Chinese dragon, with a father and mother who didn't need to breathe fire to scare the pee out of Mack.

Xiao could turn effortlessly into her current form: a pretty girl. But she insisted the other shape, the somewhat large, turquoise, snakelike form was her true self.

"Dietmar," Xiao said, "what do you think we should do?"

"Me?" Dietmar squeaked. Because he did that sometimes when Xiao talked to him. Squeak.

It was really annoying.

"Yes, Dietmar, I am asking your opinion," Xiao said patiently.

"I think we should not confront them. We should merely watch and be prepared."

"I agree," Xiao said.

"I think Stefan should go knock on their window and ask them what's up," Mack said. That was not what he had thought or said, oh, sixty seconds earlier, but it was what he thought now.

Stefan hesitated. He looked at Mack. Then he looked at Jarrah, who gave a brief nod.

The Aussie girl and Stefan had a special bond. It was the mystical bond that joined the kind of people who think it would be fun to strap rockets to bikes and fly over the Grand Canyon.

That's not some made-up example. That's from an actual conversation between Stefan and Jarrah.

Stefan swaggered over to the van and tapped on

the window with his knuckles. Mack tensed. The van window rolled down.

Stefan talked to someone, leaned in to listen, then stepped away as the window rolled back up. He came back to report to Mack.

"It's a bunch of fairies."

"Fairies?"

"Like with wings?"

"I think so," Stefan said. "They say they have a proposition."

"A proposition?" said Mack.

"That's what they said," said Stefan.

"A van full of fairies," Mack repeated.

Stefan nodded. "They want to talk to you in a safe place. Someplace neutral. That's what they said. They said there's a magical woods down the road."

That left them all staring blankly at Stefan.

"What do they want?" Jarrah asked.

Stefan shrugged. "They want Magnum bars. Five white chocolate and one Mayan Mystica. They said they're for sale in the mini-mart here. They can't go in themselves. Because, you know, they're fairies."

"We should buy them these ice-cream bars,"

Dietmar said. "Then we should talk to them and see what they want."

This was a problem for Mack because he agreed with Dietmar. But he didn't want to look like he was following Dietmar's lead. But there was no way around it: if a vanload of fairies wants to talk to you, you can't exactly blow them off.

So the Magnifica plus Stefan went in and bought the Magnum bars. Except for the Mayan Mystica because the store was out of that flavor. Stefan had to be sent back to the van to learn whether a dark chocolate would do. (Yes.)

Stefan delivered the ice cream to the fairies.

Spent at Shell station: 11.15 GBP.[4]

They waited for several minutes while, Mack assumed, the fairies ate. Then the van pulled out smoothly, and with a lurching of grinding gears, a crushed trash can, and a scream of terror from a mother pushing a stroller, Mack and his crew followed.

They drove for about a mile before pulling up in sight of Urquhart Castle, an ancient ruin that perched picturesquely beside Loch Ness. The van slowed to a

---

4 Probably about 20 dollars. Give or take.

stop in a place where there quite clearly were no woods.

The van waited and Mack and the Magnifica waited until several cars passed by. Then, when the coast was clear, the van drove straight into a stand of trees that had absolutely not been there ten seconds earlier.

Two

Mack didn't know much about trees. Unfortunately, Dietmar did.

"These are holly and rowan. Superstitious folk believe they have magical properties."

"Well, since this forest wasn't here until, like, just now, I guess maybe they're right," Mack said.

Even though the day was weakly sunny, it was dark in the woods. The van rolled to a smooth stop on a bed of fallen leaves. The car rolled into a bush, sending birds squawking away in terror. The car jerked hard a few times. Then it emitted a disgruntled farting sound and finally stopped.

The window of the van rolled down again, and out flew things sparkly and golden: the ice-cream bar wrappers.

The door opened. The fairies did not step out; they flew, six of them in all.

Having by this time been in close contact with insectoid Skirrit, treasonous Tong Elves, and disgusting Lepercons, not to mention several horrifying monsters that Risky had morphed into, Mack was ready for just about anything. So it surprised him that the fairies looked almost exactly the way he expected fairies to look.

Three were male, three were female, and all had toned little bodies clad in earthy colors. They had double wings, like dragonflies, that made a buzzing sound (again, like dragonflies) as they flew. They were all roughly the same size, each maybe half a kid in height. Or at least half a Mack. Maybe a third of a Stefan.

The surprise was not in their look: these were definitely garden-variety, standard-issue fairies. The surprise came when they opened their mouths.

"I'm Frank. This is my crew: Joey, Connie, Pete, Ellen, and Julia."

"These are not proper fairy names," Dietmar observed.

Frank squinted. "What are you, the fairy police? Our names are whatever we say they are."

But Dietmar wasn't having it. "A fairy should be named after a flower or a tree, or something in the natural world."

"And a kid should learn to keep his mouth shut," Frank snapped. And with that, he drew what had at first looked like a small sword hanging at his side. It turned out to be a droopy sort of wand.

"You like flowers? Be one," Frank said. He waved his wand and said, "*E-ma exel strel (click)haka!*"

"That's Vargran!" Jarrah said.

And Dietmar probably would have agreed except for the fact that his body had turned green and very thin. Tubular, one might even say. His arms flattened into graceful leaves. And his head formed first a tight, green bulb and then exploded outward as the petals of a magnificent-looking sunflower.

From the seedpod at the center, Dietmar's two eyes stared in shock. Frank did not seem to have bothered to give him a mouth.

Mack was torn between terror—understandable—and a feeling of glee—also understandable but not really admirable.

Xiao's eyes narrowed, and already blue scales were covering her body as she—

"Uh-uh-uh!" Frank warned, shaking his finger. "That would be a bad move, dragon girl. Your kind signed a treaty a long time ago. This is western dragon territory."

Reluctantly Xiao melted back to purely human form.

"Now, can we talk business?" Frank asked.

"You have to change Dietmar back to normal," Mack demanded, somewhat forcefully, almost as though he meant it.

"When we're done talking business."

"Okay, what business?"

Frank shot a coy look at his crew, who fluttered slightly, then settled toward the ground. The instant their bare toes touched the lush grass, their wings rolled up. Like rolling up a window shade. Just rolled up. *Whap.*

"We hear you're looking for someone," Frank said.

They were, in fact, looking for the Key. The Key to Vargran spells and curses. So far they'd found bits and pieces of Vargran, but now, as they neared the fateful confrontation to save the world from the Pale Queen, they needed more. A lot more. And the Key was . . . um . . . the key.

That's right: the Key was the key.

The Key had two parts. The first had been given to them by Nott, Norse goddess of night. And if you believed Nott (and seriously, how could you not believe a mythical Norse goddess?), the second and final part of the Key had been buried with one William Blisterthöng MacGuffin.

"Maybe," Mack said cautiously.

"No maybe about it, kid. You've been asking around about someone no one has seen in a long time. We have good sources."

Mack glanced at his companions. Jarrah shrugged.

And Mack's iPhone chimed with the tone it used to signal a message.

Mack ignored it, but it was an edgy sort of ignoring, like he was forcing himself to ignore it, which just made everyone uncomfortable, and finally Frank said,

"Oh, just go ahead and get it."

With an abashed smile, Mack pulled out his phone.

"Well? What is it?" Xiao asked impatiently.

Mack sighed. "It's my golem. He's refusing to shower in the boys' locker room."

"Lotta dudes are bashful about that," Stefan said, and no one thought he was talking about himself because Stefan was incapable of bashfulness.

"It's not about being shy," Mack said with a sigh. "He's made out of mud. That much water . . ."

"Kind of busy here," Frank interrupted impatiently. "Anyway, it's best not to coddle golems. They just get needy."

"I'll just take a minute to . . ." His words faded out as he thumbed in a response:

> You have got to handle these things yourself. You have got to be a big boy now.

"Sorry," Mack said of the interruption. "You were saying?"

"We were saying you're looking for someone who's been gone a long time."

"Let's say we are," Mack conceded. In the back of his mind he was wondering whether he'd been too harsh with the golem.

"Well, the someone you're looking for is hidden by fairy enchantment. Been hidden for more than a thousand years."

"Are we talking about the same man?" Jarrah asked.

"If it's William Blisterthöng MacGuffin, then we are talking about the same man," Frank confirmed. His eyes narrowed and his sharp little fairy teeth showed behind tightened lips. "And you'll never find him. Never! Never . . . without our help."

"Why would you help us?" Mack asked.

Frank shrugged. "A friend of ours wants something in return. Something you might be able to get for her. One hand washes the other. I scratch your back, you scratch mine. Tit for tat."

"Can we stop being cryptic, please, and get to the point?" Xiao asked politely. "My friend is not happy as a flower."

Dietmar was unhappy with good reason—a pair of crows came swooping down and lit on Dietmar's huge petals and began to pick at the seeds.

"Hey, hey, get out of here!" Jarrah waved them off,

but they retreated only as far as a low tree branch and from there kept a close eye on Dietmar's sunflower seeds.

"You tell the tale, Connie—you tell it best." Frank indicated one of the female fairies, a dark-haired, dark-eyed, tiny little beauty in a deep-green formfitting outfit.

"How do you suppose MacGuffin came to be called Blisterthöng?" Connie asked rhetorically in an enchanting fairy voice. She kind of writhed or danced as she spoke. It was a sort of dramatic interpretation: she used sweeping hand gestures, and sometimes lowered her head in sadness, or threw open her arms to show joy. "For many long years after the Romans left, and after the druids faded, and as the new faith was coming to Scotland, the fairies lived in peace. We are a peaceable folk. No fairy has ever raised a hand in violence against another!" She made a very dramatic upraised-fist move on that last line.

Mack nodded thoughtfully because that seemed like the thing to do.

"Except for the Seventeen Year War," Pete the fairy interjected.

"And the War of the Sweltering Cave," Julia added

helpfully. "And the Rabid Peace of Kilcannon's Bluff."

"With those few exceptions, no fairy had ever raised a hand in violence against another," Connie reiterated, again with the upraised fist of forcefulness. "Unless you're going to count the Battle of the Pretenders."

"Or the Flaming Disagreement," Frank said.

"Or the Pantsing of Fain's Firth."

"Or the Castle-Whacking Unpleasantness."

"Or O'Toole's Tools of Terror."

"Or the War of the Noses."

They went on like this for quite a while. And Mack began to wonder if the fairies were exaggerating their peacefulness.

"Or the Frightful Fruit Fight."[5]

"Or Little Dora's Comeuppance."

Finally, after about ten minutes, they ran out of wars, skirmishes, misunderstandings, slaughters, backstabbings, and murdering peaces, and Connie got back to her main theme, which was, "Aside from those few[6] minor matters, no fairy has ever raised a hand in violence against another."

---

5 If you're reading this aloud, you may want to try that again.

6 Two hundred and seventy-six. It would have been two hundred and seventy-seven, but they overlooked the Intentional Infliction of Ignominy at Inverness.

Fist for emphasis.

"Until . . . ," Frank interjected with great drama and a dramatic flourish of his wand.

"Until William MacGuffin stole the Key and used it to take sides with the fairies of clan Gorse against clan Begonia."

A strangled sound—much like a high-pitched human voice coming from inside a flower—came from the giant sunflower. Lacking lips, tongue, or teeth, Dietmar had a hard time expressing himself clearly, but it was something like, "See! I told you so. Those are flower names!"

Mack ignored him and waited for Connie to finish her story.

The crows looked speculatively, wondering if they could make a quick in-and-out dash. Some seeds, maybe a little eyeball . . .

"MacGuffin wanted gold, and as you know, fairies have plenty of it," Connie said. "So for thirty pieces of gold MacGuffin gave the Gorse King new and more dangerous Vargran curses. Curses that gave the Gorse King power over the Begonias and our beloved All-Mother."

"Is there any way we can hurry this along?" Jarrah

complained. "I'm beginning to regret we didn't eat those ice-cream bars ourselves."

"MacGuffin helped the Gorse to formulate a terrible, terrible curse." Connie made an interesting move here, jabbing her hands forward away from her mouth, like stabbing finger-tongues. "It was a curse that caused a hideous rash in the form of rose thorns to grow in the sensitive parts of a fairy body."

"Yeesh," Mack said, and winced.

"Ah," Xiao said, nodding her head almost as smugly as Dietmar sometimes did. "Hence the name *Blisterthöng.*"

"For a thousand years we of clan Begonia have thirsted after his blood so that we might have our revenge," Frank said, shaking his little peace-loving fist and baring his sharp peace-loving teeth.

"Because of your peaceful nature and all," Mack said dryly. "We thought MacGuffin was dead. It's been a thousand years."

"No, he's not dead. He's concealed by a powerful spell of the Gorse King. His castle is invisible to human eyes. Only those with the *enlightened puissance*—and few humans possess it—can see him or his castle."

"That's why you need us."

"Yes, Mack of the Magnifica. You and these others—but not you," Frank said, pointing out Stefan, who shuffled in embarrassment, "possess the *enlightened puissance*. I can make it possible for you to see the Concealed Castle of MacGuffin. And I can make it possible for you to see the All-Mother, whom only a few have seen before. And even fewer have photographed. You must take the Key from MacGuffin. And you must swear to free the All-Mother from the Gorse King's spell."

"Wait, I'm losing track," Jarrah said. "This All-Mother of yours has the Blisterthöng rash?"

The fairies looked at her like she was an idiot. Which Mack thought was unfair since he had wondered the same thing.

"No. Duh," Frank said. "She's trapped in the body of a sea serpent."

It took a moment for the reality to percolate up through Mack's brain. Don't blame him for being a little slow. He was very bright, and very attentive, but already the day had involved near death-by-car-accident and a vanful of fairies. So if he was a little slow, hey, give him a break.

"Are you talking about the Loch Ness monster?" Mack asked.

Frank bridled a bit at that, unfurled his wings, and rose a few feet into the air. "She is Eimhur Ceana Una Mordag, All-Mother to clan Begonia, as well as Beloved of the Gods, the Ultimate Warrioress, and a past holder of the record for longest sustained note on the bagpipes—they say many who heard were driven mad." Then he settled himself down and, with a shrug, said, "But yes, most know her as the Loch Ness monster."

"Well then," Jarrah said briskly, "magic castle, some old dead fart who makes fairies get rashes, and the Loch Ness monster: all in a day's work."

Three

MEANWHILE, AT RICHARD GERE MIDDLE SCHOOL[7]

The golem stared at the phone. The message from Mack was very clear.

> You have got to handle these things yourself. You have got to be a big boy now.

---

7 Go, Fighting Pupfish!

Yes. As usual, Mack had the right answer.

It was amazing, really, how right Mack was about, well, everything.

Clearly if the golem was a "big boy" then he could survive the shower. How much bigger? That was the question.

The golem began to text this question to Mack, but then stopped himself. You have got to handle these things yourself.

Yes, that was true, he supposed: responsibility. He would have to work it out himself.

Morning at school was always a confusing time for the golem. There were so many kids rushing this way and that, many saying, "Hi," or, "Hey, weirdo," or, "Get out of my way, you freak." He tried to be pleasant to each and smile or say, "How are you today?" But it was hectic. Especially on days when Matthew Morgan would chain him to the bike rack or Camaro Angianelli would throw him into the bushes.

The golem didn't quite understand what was going

www.themag12.com

32

on—he was passing as Mack but he didn't quite have Mack's brains—but it seemed there was a sort of bully war going on at Richard Gere Middle School.[8] Since Mack had left and taken Stefan Marr with him, the carefully negotiated bully peace had broken down.

Stefan had enforced peace among bullies by working out a complex system of assigned victims. Thus, under Stefan's regime, there had been a bully for nerds, a bully for geeks, a bully for stoners, a bully for emo kids, a goths' bully, a skaters' bully, a rich kids' bully—each bully with his or her own population of victims.

And of course one bully to rule them all, one bully to bind them, one bully to bring them all and in the darkness pound them. Which would be Stefan.

That system had worked surprisingly well. It kept kids from being "overbullied." It wasn't like just any bully could push a nerd around—only the designated bully of nerds could do that. And Stefan had established some limits. He had even conducted a bullying seminar, laying out what was and what was not acceptable bully behavior.

Yep. Those were the good old days.

---

8 Go, Fighting Pupfish!

Now, with the King of the Bullies off saving the world with Mack, everything was chaos. Suddenly bullies were trying to expand beyond their usual victim group. The emo bully had tried to claim that anyone who went to Hot Topic was, by definition, one of his rightful victims. This was opposed strongly by Ed Lafrontiere—the current *Twilight* fans' bully—and this had set off a power struggle as various bullies tried to take over the title of King of the Bullies (or in the case of Camaro Angianelli, Queen).

Somehow the intrabully war had resulted in a sort of competition to see who could be the biggest bully to Mack. Or in fact: the golem.

His mom usually drove him to school in the morning. If by *his mom*, you meant Mack's mom. The golem didn't really have a mother, or a father. This was the first time in his brief life he'd had any sort of family, and they weren't really his.

The golem had been formed and given life by Grimluk. He had suddenly opened his eyes in a tiny stone house on a distant hillside in . . . well, now that he thought about it, the golem wasn't really sure where it was. Not around here, anyway.

He had begun to achieve consciousness when

his head was formed. He had opened his eyes to see Grimluk's ancient, grizzled, wrinkled, rheumy-eyed face staring down at him. Grimluk's gnarled fingers had literally smoothed the mud that made the golem's forehead.

The golem had blinked and looked around, confused. He was in some ways no different from a newborn baby.

He had looked down to see that his body was nothing but some tree branches—bark still on for better mud adherence[9]—tied together with rattan to form a sort of bare scarecrow form.

There was a massive wooden tub full of mud. And a smaller crockery pot with more sticks and loops of rattan.

"I'm getting too old for this," Grimluk had muttered.

"Mama?" the golem had asked, gazing up hopefully.

"No, fool. You're a golem. You have neither father nor mother. You have a maker. That's me."

"I . . . I feel like . . . like we should hug," the golem had said.

Grimluk had been somewhat taken aback by this.

---

9 This is a helpful hint for when you go to build your own golem.

But after he'd harrumphed a bit and chewed on his lip and forgotten what he was doing a few times and made some grunting noises and scratched and hitched up his robe, he'd finally said, "Eh? Let's shake hands."

Then after Grimluk had packed mud onto the golem's stick arm and stuck in five twigs to act as supports for fingers and then carefully formed the hand, the golem had shaken hands with his maker.

"What's my name?" the golem had asked.

"You don't have one. Until I place the scroll in your mouth—and then you'll know what part you are to play in the great events that rush toward us like an enraged boar."

"What's an enraged boar?"

"An angry wild pig."

"What's a pig?"

Grimluk was not a great teacher. The golem never did find out what a boar was. But Grimluk was a good golem maker.

When at last the golem was completed and stood on his own two muddy feet, Grimluk smiled a toothless smile. "All right, then."

The golem had watched, mystified but also

hopeful, as the elderly Magnifica, the sole surviving member of the first Magnificent Twelve, wrote two words on a slip of parchment.

The words were "Be Mack."

"I don't understand," the golem said.

"You will," Grimluk said. "Open your mouth and stick out your tongue."

"What's a mouth?"

Grimluk helped him understand that. Then he placed the scroll on the golem's tongue.

What magic then!

The transformation was miraculous. The creature of mud and twigs suddenly had skin. He had eyes with whites and colored irises. He had hair. Fingernails.

Now, granted, Grimluk had sort of glossed over the internal organs—the golem would have to dig some of those out himself—but the result was a creature that looked very much like Mack MacAvoy.

So much like Mack that Mack's best friends—those who knew him really well—were only a little suspicious. And his parents never guessed at all.

And then, he had met Mack face-to-face. A real human boy. The boy he was to be for however long it took Mack to save the world.

That had been kind of wonderful, meeting Mack.

But right now, here, today, he had no time for more nostalgia. He had to be a big boy now.

The question was: just how big?

He looked down and noticed that the mud-passing-as-flesh was oozing out over the tops of his shoes. And his jeans were already tight.

Yep: time to be a big boy.

Four

William Blisterthöng MacGuffin's castle turned out to be right there in the open atop a sheer outcropping, less than a quarter mile from Urquhart Castle, which was right beside Loch Ness.

Frank had chanted a Vargran spell over the Magnifica and Stefan, and the castle had appeared in perfect clarity. Big as life.

Then the fairies had urged them forward with encouraging words.

"Wait, you're not coming with us?" Mack demanded.

"This could get violent," Frank pointed out, "and we are peaceable folk."

"No fairy has ever—" Connie started in, and Xiao, who was usually very polite, said, "Yeah, right."

Over the years rare individuals who possessed just a little of the *enlightened puissance* had caught vague, fleeting glimpses of the castle. But when they reported this, they were condemned as drunk or crazy. Or as crazy drunks.

It was even worse for those few who would also report having seen a sort of sea serpent swimming around in Loch Ness. Those people were also derided as drunk or crazy or both, plus they were often compelled to write books and set up websites in a desperate attempt to prove that they were right.

They were right. But merely writing a book doesn't prove you're sane or sober (more the opposite).

Here's what the local folk and passersby saw as Mack, Jarrah, Xiao, Stefan, and a nonflowery and rather annoyed Dietmar climbed the incredibly steep face of the hill: nothing. That's what. Once Mack and the gang had come within a hundred feet of the massive promontory (there's a word to dazzle your teacher with), they simply slipped from view. A person watching from the road would have seen five kids crossing a field and passing beneath a small stand of stunted trees, and then . . . nothing.

And here is what Stefan saw: also nothing. Because although Stefan had many great qualities, like, um . . . toughness and dangerousness . . . he did not possess the *enlightened puissance*. In fact, as far as Stefan could tell, the rest of them were crazy people gazing up at nothing.

This made it very difficult for Stefan to climb. He could feel the ground under his feet, he could even climb, but it was sketchy work. Try climbing something you can't see. Go ahead, try. The story can wait.

See? It's not easy, is it?

The climb was mostly over tumbled boulders. At some point back in history, the side of the mountain had crumbled. The other sides were all still nearly vertical cliff. But this side offered some possibilities for ascent.

So Jarrah held Stefan's hand and guided him every step of the way with comments like, "Here you go, upsy-daisy, eh?" And, "Come on then, mate, just jump it." And, "Nah, you won't fall more than twenty feet, and that's nothing."

"I could fly up there in two seconds," Xiao muttered. "Stupid treaties. Like I would be any kind of threat to those big, leathery, murderous, fire-breathing western dragons."

"Still, it is a sort of law," Dietmar said. "And we must obey the law."

That remark seemed to lessen Xiao's affection for Dietmar substantially. Xiao could get a very hard look in her eyes and set a very determined jaw when you annoyed her.

Mack brought up the rear, stepping cautiously and gazing up anxiously every few seconds to see just how little progress they had made. It was also his job as the leader to think of a plan for dealing with MacGuffin once they found him. So far his plan was to ask him very politely if they could have the Key, and would he mind releasing the Begonia clan's All-Mother.

He did have one other idea. He yelled to Jarrah, who was at that moment in midair between boulders. "Jarrah, make sure your mom gets you the latest Vargran."

"Done," Jarrah said. She landed like a cat, stood up, pulled out her iPhone, and pointed to it with her free hand. "Nothing new: Mother is on holiday with Dad." Then she was knocked over by Stefan, who had come to kind of like jumping over invisible boulders. From his point of view he was climbing in midair.

Vargran was the magical language, long forgotten, and only really useful to those very few who were born with the *enlightened puissance*. Jarrah's mother was an archaeologist in Australia, where she had discovered some bits and pieces of Vargran carved into a cave wall inside the massive rock known as Uluru.

So far they had learned that Vargran had sounds that included a throat-clearing sound (*ch*), a click, and a sniff, as well as more normal consonants and vowels. And they had learned that Vargran had four basic verb forms: infinitive, past, future, and or else.

Generally magical spells involved the "or else" tense, which added a *ma* on the end.

To date they had used Vargran to make a small sun, to cause blue-cheese-filled Lepercons to grow, and to go shopping at Harrods department store, although they hadn't really intended that last one.

The whole experience had not been very satisfying. Which was why they needed the Key. With MacGuffin's key matched to the earlier piece of the key—the part they'd obtained from the goddess Nott—they would be able to learn a whole lot more Vargran. The language was, after all, their only weapon, and they didn't have a lot of time left to assemble the rest of the twelve, somehow convince the traitorous Magnifica Valin to switch sides, and stop the Pale Queen. They needed Vargran. And no: there was no app for that.

About halfway up the mountain they had a lucky break: a stairway, carved into the cliff face. It had once gone all the way down, but when the mountain collapsed, so had the bottom half of the staircase—a fact that made Mack a bit nervous as he climbed his weary way up the narrow, overly tall steps.

It was a good thing they found the stairs because the sun was setting and casting very long, deep shadows all around them, turning every jagged rock into a monster's head. (Not literally, that was a simile. Or possibly a metaphor. One of those.)

The staircase ended in a stone guardhouse. To their immense relief there was a fountain spouting what they fervently hoped was water. It wasn't warm in Scotland, but it was humid, and they were all sweating and huffing and puffing, so they plopped down on stone benches, cupped water with their hands and drank, and gazed out across the landscape below: the road, Urquhart Castle, and the loch beyond.

Mack caught Stefan's eye, and the two of them went to take a look up at MacGuffin's castle. Darkness was falling fast. It was autumn in Scotland, when days are short and nights are long.

The castle was in perfect repair, not a ruin like Urquhart, which looked as ancient as it was. This castle looked as if it had just been built last week. The stone was clean and lichen-free. The mortar was all fresh. Even the grass below the walls looked green and new-mown.

Also, the row of skulls used to outline the massive timber door was impeccable. They stood out white against dark stone.

"Any way we can sneak in?" Mack wondered aloud.

"I can't see anything," Stefan pointed out. "It's like I'm standing in the air looking at a cloud."

"Ah. Right. Well, it's got high walls, a couple of

giant towers, and a massive wooden gate."

"Human pyramid?" Stefan said, and for a moment Mack wasn't entirely sure it was stupid.

"The walls are too high," Mack said regretfully. "We need him to open the door. We need a diversion. We need him to come out after some of us while the rest sneak in and find the Key."

Then, suddenly, without warning, came a sound so terrible Mack felt as if his blood had frozen solid in his veins.

Bleeeeeaaaat-skurrrreeeeeeeeee-waaahhhhhh!

"Oh my God, what is that?" Xiao cried. She had come running. "It sounds as if a goat is being tortured!"

"It sounds like all the pain in existence since the dawn of time!" Jarrah said.

"It sounds like the cry of a newborn demon ready to destroy all peace and love!" Dietmar said. "But I believe it is merely a bagpipe."

"Oh, yeah," Mack said. "A bagpipe. I was going to guess that."

"So, who is going to be the diversion?" Jarrah asked after Mack described his plan, which wasn't really much of a plan.

"You know . . . ," Mack said, stroking his chin thoughtfully. "Something just occurred to me: maybe the door isn't locked. I mean, it's not like he gets many visitors up here. Why would he lock a door no one has come to in a thousand years?"

So they crept forward in single file with Mack in the lead. The bagpipe did not play again. There was a deep silence everywhere and the stars were beginning to blink on in the dark blue sky overhead.

The door was about ten feet tall, maybe eight feet wide, and made of wood that looked like it could be two feet thick. It was the kind of door Mack wished he had on his room. Maybe without the skulls grinning down. That was a little too much.

There wasn't a handle, really, or a knocker or a bell. So Mack simply pushed on the wood where a handle might have been.

Instantly the bagpipe screeched, and this time that horrifying sound was joined by a chorus of shrill, high-pitched voices. It sounded like a church choir of toddlers cranked up on soda and Smarties trying to sing along with a howling devil.

"Interesting doorbell, eh?" Jarrah said. She was

acting tough, but the noise had scared them all. All except Stefan, who yelled, "Hey, shut up!"

The chorus was instantly silenced. The door moved on its own, slowly widening the gap.

Mack was pretty sure duty required him to be the first one through, but fortunately Stefan pushed ahead. Stefan wasn't good at fear. He just didn't seem to get it. Even when he couldn't see anything but the night sky.

Mack was right behind him, shoulder to shoulder with Jarrah, with Dietmar and Xiao following closely. They formed a little knot of scared kids.

The door slammed behind them.

They found themselves in a dark courtyard. Only the faint starlight revealed tall, crenellated walls and arches, with hard-on-the-feet cobblestones underfoot.

"Hey! I can see it now," Stefan said. The spell of invisibility only worked on the exterior of the castle, like a coat of camouflage.

"Um . . . ," Mack said.

Before he could finish his thought (and we'll never know what it was), a torch burst into wild orange flame. It was about eye level on the wall to their right.

Then a second torch. Another. Another.

A line of torches moved from right to left, turned the corner to cross the facing wall, then came around to trace the left wall.

The torches whipped frantically as though they were in a strong wind, but it was perfectly still in the courtyard.

In the flickering orange glow they could see quite clearly. Yes, there were tall walls all around. And gloomy arches outlined in gleaming white skulls. Mack noticed—because Mack noticed things—that not all of the skulls were human. There were some that were too small to be human. There were others too large, far too large, and with teeth where teeth had no business being.

Against the facing wall, flanked on both sides by shadowed arches, a rough-hewn throne sat atop a platform. And on that throne sat a man. He was wearing a skirt. And every one of the Magnifica and Stefan had the identical thought: I hope that dude keeps his legs crossed.

The man was built as wide as he was tall, but he was still plenty tall. He had extravagant red hair pushing out from beneath a too-small cap. His massive hands gripped the arms of the throne as if he would—and could—rip them right off at any moment.

He stared with eyes that glittered from deep, torch-cast shadows.

"I am the MacGuffin," he announced in a heavily accented speech. "Wha urr ye, 'n' how have you come 'ere uninvited?"

The stones seemed to shake when he spoke. Or maybe it was just that Mack shook. Mack was not fond of beards. In fact, he suffered from pogonophobia—an irrational fear of beards, which only distance could keep under control.

"We're, um . . . ," Mack began, before faltering. He glanced aside and happened to see Dietmar. Somehow now Dietmar wasn't all that interested in taking the lead. "We're, um, hikers. Is this Urquhart Castle? Because that's . . . that's where we . . . um . . ."

"Urquhart Castle, is it?" MacGuffin demanded, and gnashed his teeth. "Di ah keek lik' a Durward?"

"A what?"

"A Durward!" MacGuffin shouted.

"What's a Durward?"

"Th' Durwards ur th' family that runs Urquhart Castle, ye ninny."

Dietmar got a crafty look on his face. "Shouldn't

Urquhart Castle be run by a family named Urquhart?"

"Na, you great eejit!"

Dietmar did not like being called a "great eejit" so soon after suffering the indignity of being transformed into a sunflower. And, as Mack noticed grudgingly, Dietmar had some spine. The German boy was not a wimp, and he was getting ready to say something forceful to MacGuffin.

But there was something crazy in MacGuffin's eyes, which perfectly reflected the light of the torches from under bushy eyebrows, and Dietmar chose to do the wise thing and fall silent.

MacGuffin leaned forward and glared at Mack. "Ah ken how come yer 'ere. Ye huv come tae steal mah key."

"Key?" Mack said disingenuously. "What key?"

"Dinnae tak' me fur a gowk. Ye huv th' *enlightened puissance* or ye wouldn't be 'ere. Ah ken th' Pale Queen rises, wee jimmy. Ah ken wha 'n' whit yer."

Or, in regular English, "Don't take me for a fool. You have the *enlightened puissance* or you wouldn't be here. I know the Pale Queen rises, boy. I know who and what you are."

And it was at that heart-stopping moment that

Mack's phone made an eerie sound. The sound of an incoming text message.

Slowly . . . slooooowly . . . cautiously . . . Mack drew out his iPhone.

MacGuffin stared at the oblong object in Mack's hand. Stared at it as if he was seeing a ghost.

"Whit's that black magic?" MacGuffin demanded in cringing horror.

See, that's the problem with being stuck in an invisible castle for a thousand years: you miss out on a lot of new technology.

Mack did the thing that really should have saved his life. "This!" he cried, holding up the phone and glancing at the message—which was from the golem, and which said, "Pocket lint is tasty"—"Is the mighty iMagic of . . . of Appletonia! If you harm me or my friends, I will use it to destroy you!"

Five

MEANWHILE, AT RICHARD GERE MIDDLE SCHOOL[10]

Thousands of miles away, Mack's golem was eating lint from his pocket and growing larger. The lint happened to be mostly blue because he was wearing blue jeans, but there was some white as well. For variety. And it had a lingering flavor of garlic because, while Mack's mom had washed these jeans

---

10 Heck yeah, we're doing it: Go, Fighting Pupfish!

after the golem misunderstood the name Hot Pockets and stuffed a microwaved pizza-flavored Hot Pocket into his pocket, some of that flavor had survived.

When Grimluk tapped Mack to go off and save the world, he gave him the golem to fill in for him at home. The golem now looked exactly like Mack, albeit somewhat muddier, and quite a bit less, um, how to put this gently?

Um . . . okay: Mack was a pretty smart guy. His golem? Not as smart. There: it's been said.

So the golem attended Mack's school and took Mack's classes and wrote Mack's papers. His latest effort, six pages on the history topic "Maybe Abraham Lincoln Had Mice Living in His Beard," had consisted entirely of the sentence, "He could have, no one knows," written in various fonts and in various type sizes. On page four, for example, the font was so large that the entire page just read, "HE COULD HA."

It's a good thing all that stuff about a "permanent record" is just something made up by teachers. Because the golem had caused Mack's steady B+ average to drop somewhat.

The only class where the golem was actually

outperforming Mack was gym. He was helped by his ability to physically absorb dodgeballs, draw them into his body, unhinge his jaw, and shoot them back out of his mouth at supersonic speed.

He had an A+ in gym.

And if there was a dodgeball team choosing sides, the golem was always picked first.

The only problem the golem had with gym was the showering part. Water had a tendency to wash him away. Imagine mud. Now imagine mud with a sort of coating of fleshlike paint. Now imagine streaming hot water. You can see the problem for yourself. A kid had once caught sight of the golem's face after a shower, and that kid now lives with his father in another state.

Where he sees a therapist three times a week.

And wakes up screaming.

But! If there were more golem to begin with, the water wouldn't be able to wash him all down the drain. It would wash some of him away, sure, and that could be pretty unsightly. But if he were a really big boy, the water would only damage a tiny bit of him.

That was math, and the golem liked math.

In addition to school, the golem also filled in for

Mack at home. He performed all of Mack's important family duties: finding the remote control, nodding solemnly during parental lectures, pretending to do homework, wearing the same socks every day for weeks, taking out the trash after being asked exactly seventeen times, and heatedly pointing out examples of parental hypocrisy. Such as, "You say don't eat the leather sofa cushions but you eat bacon, which is the same as leather!"

There were days when Mack was ambivalent about saving the world, because if he did, he'd sooner or later end up back in Sedona with a lot of explaining to do.

And there were times when the golem had just the most fleeting thought[11] that if Mack succeeded and returned to reclaim his life, it would be the end of a very happy time for the golem.

He wasn't sure what happened to golems after they completed a mission. Maybe he would be sent off to "be" someone else.

Then again, maybe he would just return to being unconscious mud and twigs.

Meanwhile, the golem was showing up for school, pacifying Mack's parents, and kind of dating Camaro

---

11 All his thoughts were fleeting.

Angianelli, one of the bullies at Richard Gere Middle School (Go, Fighting Pupfish!).

Camaro found the golem very sensitive and insightful and an amazing dancer. And no one could take a punch like the golem.

She was punching him right now, in fact, as he changed classes. "You look like you're putting on weight," Camaro said. And she punched him in the stomach to illustrate. Her fist went all the way in, all the way up to the leather bracelet on her wrist, before bouncing back out.

"Yes. I am going to be a big boy," the golem said.

Camaro looked up at him speculatively. "Are you any good at punching people out? Because when I make my play for supreme bully power and try to take over Stefan's old job, I could use a big boy backing me up."

"I will be big," the golem confirmed, and grinned.

"You have a twig in your teeth," Camaro pointed out.

"Yes. I do," the golem said proudly.

"I like that about you, Mack: you rock your own special style. No one else has twigs in their teeth. It's a built-in toothpick."

The golem had to think about that for a moment

before finally saying, "Yes."

"So," Camaro whispered conspiratorially. "Sometime within the next few days, it's me and Tony Pooch at the usual place." She cracked her knuckles, flexed the biceps displayed by her sleeveless T-shirt, gave her neck the old, familiar Stefan Marr warm-up twist, and spit a wad of gum at a passing geek.

"You're going out with Tony Pooch?" The golem was bothered by this. He enjoyed spending time with Camaro—he found her random destructiveness charming. He almost felt jealous. Yes. Almost.

Camaro threw back her head and laughed. Then she gave him an affectionate punch in the arm—a punch that would have reduced anyone else to whimpering and a possible blood clot—and said, "No, no, Mack. I mean I'm going to kick his butt."

"Ah."

"I'm your girl," Camaro said affectionately, and followed that statement up with a snarling warning that he had better never forget it. Not if he wanted to keep all four of his limbs.

He did want to keep all four of his limbs because it was crucial to passing as Mack. Coming home without an arm would definitely generate uncomfortable questions from Mom. And if he lost two or more limbs, even Dad might notice.

"You're my girl," the golem said contentedly. "And I'm your big boy."

Mack was going to have a lot of explaining to do when he got home.

But at the moment the golem had given him an opportunity. . . .

Six

"I am the Wizard of the iPhone!" Mack cried, sounding a little desperate. "Gaze upon this and be afraid, William Blisterthöng MacGuffin! Behold, as I kill a pig using only an angry bird!"

MacGuffin sat back hard when he saw that. Then he leaned forward to look closer, because the screen was pretty small. But Mack could see the fear in the old ginger's eyes.

"I, too, am a wizard!" Jarrah cried, getting into the act. "I can make nanobots take over a human brain!"

"And I can look up words and translate them from German to English!" Dietmar announced.

This assault of smartphones baffled and amazed the thousand-year-old man. In MacGuffin's world the very height of technology was the windmill, the crossbow, and something very new and exciting: the fork.

He had never seen a phone, let alone a phone that contained tiny people within it and could play music. From his point of view, Mack and his friends were indeed magicians. Wizards! Who else could cause rectangular lights to appear in their palms? Who else could plant tiny crops of wheat and corn inside that rectangle of light? Who else could reveal pictures of themselves playing volleyball at their cousin's birthday party?

"Give us the Key, William Blisterthöng MacGuffin, or we will unleash the power of the iMagic to shrink you to the size of one of these captive pigs, and we will pelt you with the angriest of birds!"

Mack put that out there in his deepest, most impressive voice, and he wore his most serious and solemn expression.

And it would have worked. Maybe.

Except that something like a very large dragonfly

suddenly zipped into the torchlight.

"It's a trick," Connie the fairy said. "Don't believe them, Willy."

MacGuffin leaped from his chair. He stood there and stared, stared hard like he was seeing the end of the world or maybe like he was seeing something impossible or maybe like he was seeing another *Transformers* sequel and just not believing it.

His mouth moved but no sounds came out.

And then a single great sob.

"Con?" he said through quivering mustachioed (top and bottom) lips.

"Yes, Willy, it's me. It's me, your Connie."

"Efter a' thae lang years, mah yin true loue?"

Which, to the amazement of absolutely everyone, even Stefan, meant, "After all these long years, my one true love?"

The fairy flew—that's not a metaphor, she flew— to him and wrapped her arms around his hairy red head, and MacGuffin lifted a massive paw with amazing gentleness to cradle her tiny face.

"Willy, this is all Frank's doing," Connie said, and made the fist of forcefulness again. "He's shown them the way to take the Key. In exchange, they've sworn to release the All-Mother."

"She wha haes vowed tae string a fiddle wi' mah tendons, then speil a jolly tune 'n' dae a jig?"

("She who has vowed to string a fiddle with my tendons, then play a jolly tune and do a jig?")

"Aye, my love," Connie said, stroking his Gandalf eyebrows.

They gazed into each other's eyes with the tenderest of love. Such love.

With sinking heart, Mack faced the terrible truth: Connie had betrayed her fellow fairies.

Which was pretty heinous.

But of far greater concern to Mack was that she'd also pulled the rug out from under him and his friends.

"Seize them!" William Blisterthöng MacGuffin roared.

At first this didn't trouble Mack too much because he hadn't seen any minions who might do any seizing. But he soon saw that he had simply lacked imagination. Because the skulls set above the archways—human and not-human—suddenly creaked and groaned and opened their jaws. Yellow torchlight leaped into the empty eye sockets. And, to Mack's infinite horror, the skulls began to grow necks and shoulders in the very stone of the walls.

Let's make this clear: the stone itself seemed to soften, to liquefy, and from that gooey stone emerged skeletons, like dinosaur bones rising up out of a tar pit, or Upper East Side society women emerging from the mud bath at the spa.

The hair on Mack's head stood up.

Stefan went in swinging. He punched the first skeleton so hard the skull went flying like a penalty kick.

But in a heartbeat three other skeletons—a human, something that looked like it might have been a wolf, and something else that looked like it had too many hands and a partial exoskeleton—bore him down to the paving stones with kicks and jabs.

"*Ret-ma belast!*" Mack cried. Which in Vargran is, "Stop, monsters!"

This worked, but only a little. About a quarter of the skeletons stopped dead. Well, stopped, anyway. The rest kept right on coming.

"Thay aren't a' monsters, ye wee twit," MacGuffin chortled.

Jarrah had leaped to Stefan's defense and was hauling back on skulls, and Xiao had raced to grab a torch from its sconce and was now swinging it around her so fast it was like a circle of fire.

Dietmar grabbed Mack's arm. "We need more Vargran!"

"*Ret-ma* . . . um . . . What's the word for *man*?"

"*Dood!*" Dietmar supplied.

"*Ret-ma dood!*" Mack cried, and at that instant a skeletal fist that had closed around his neck froze. Unfortunately, it froze in place. It froze choking Mack's throat.

Mack's eyes began to bulge. He grabbed the skeletal human arm and yanked it wildly back and forth. The elbow snapped and the arm came loose. The grip stayed tight, so Mack twirled and gagged with a bony hand around his neck and a bony arm sticking out, and it's amazing how quickly choking will drop you to your knees.

The world was swimming around Mack and he knew his time was measured in seconds.

Suddenly, there was Dietmar getting his fingers around the skeletal thumb and pulling just hard enough to let a few pumps of blood reach Mack's buzzy brain.

But then whatever skeletons weren't either monster or human knocked Dietmar to the ground.

Jarrah now had a torch of her own and was stabbing it into weird rib cages and up under bony jaws, and Xiao copied that action, and it seemed that, dead though they might be, the bony creatures didn't like that much.

The Magnifica had used Vargran to stop about half the skeletons, and with their fists and torches they were holding their own . . . until.

Until MacGuffin seized a massive cudgel—a stick with a gnarled knob of polished wood on one end— and came wading into the fight.

He jabbed the stick with amazing force into Stefan's chest. Stefan staggered back, clutched at his chest, sucked air, and landed on his back.

Seeing him down, the remaining skeletons regrouped. They pulled back, bunched together, and came on in a rush.

Mack was still struggling with the bony hand around his throat, still gasping for air.

Xiao, Dietmar, and Jarrah took the worst of it and

all three were down in seconds, buried by a tangle of clacking bones.

MacGuffin strode over to Mack, who was still very much in danger of passing out.

"Gimme up tae th' All-Mother, wull ye?" He grabbed a handful of Mack's curls and looked hard into Mack's bulging, tear-streaming eyes. "Na, ah think ah will murdurr ye 'n' then see howfur this rabble o' yers likes it."

Connie zipped over, fast as a hummingbird but twice as mean. She had a coil of rope, and a weakened, gagging Mack could do nothing to stop being hog-tied.

MacGuffin pried the skeletal hand from Mack's throat. A heap of bones assembled itself back into a proper skeleton and came over to retrieve the missing limb.

Oxygen flooded Mack's lungs, and his delirious brain refocused in time to see the skeleton army marching the Magnifica and Stefan to the gate of the castle, beaten, humiliated, and helpless.

Mack himself was taken to the dungeon.

Seven

Have you ever seen a dungeon? They aren't happy places. Down toward the foundation, the castle was built of massive blocks of granite, each of them about six feet by four feet.

Those stones weren't going anywhere.

The dungeons were cells, with damp stone walls covered in lichen and mold and mildew and moss. But the lichen, etc.—that's not what bothered Mack. He had no great fear of primitive plant phyla.

In the corner of the cell was a cracked pottery jar

that was supposed to be the toilet. At some later point, one of MacGuffin's skeletal helpers would be coming by to collect whatever was in the chamber pot—and really, there were never going to be good surprises there—but that was not what bothered Mack.

Well, it bothered him a little bit, because like most of us he was fond of indoor plumbing. But none of the terrors and inconveniences compared to the thing that really bothered him.

Three stone walls, a stone ceiling, a great stone floor—and the remaining wall of the cube was a sheet of rusty black iron pierced only by the door, which was itself massively iron. In that door was a single narrow vertical slit no more than six inches high and one inch wide, just enough for a skeletal eye to appear occasionally and spy in on Mack.

Not that even a skeletal eye could see much, because it was very dark in the room. There was an oil lamp set into the wall. The lamp itself would have been kind of a cute Halloween decoration: a skull with a jaw that worked like a drawer. The jaw-drawer could be pulled out, and inside would be found the little clay cup that held the reeking oil. When lit, the dim light flickered through the eyeholes and noseholes and the fine cracks where the plates of the skull were joined, and also the jagged hole where the crossbow bolt had long ago pierced the skull's brain.

But even that wasn't what terrified Mack, and overwhelmed him, and stripped away his dignity and his self-control.

What bothered Mack was a little thing called claustrophobia.

Mack had twenty-one identified phobias. They included arachnophobia, a fear of spiders.

Dentophobia, a fear of dentists.

Pyrophobia, a fear of fire, although most people have some of that.

Pupaphobia, a fear of puppets. But he was not afraid of clowns, unlike most sensible people.

Vaccinophobia, a fear of getting shots.

Thalassophobia, a fear of oceans, which led fairly naturally to selachophobia, a fear of sharks.

And of course, phobophobia, which is the fear of developing more fears. Someone famous—either Franklin D. Roosevelt or possibly SpongeBob—once said, "The only thing we have to fear is fear itself."

Well, that wasn't the only thing Mack had to fear, but it was one of them.

But the mother of all fears for Mack was claustrophobia: a fear of small, enclosed spaces. For example: a cramped space not that much bigger than a casket in the stony bowels of a castle. Because the cell was not the large room you've been picturing in your head. It was five feet deep, three feet wide, and four feet tall.

Mack could not even stand all the way up.

If he lay down on the hard stone floor, his feet would touch the door and his head would touch the far wall. And he would be able to press his hands against both side walls.

He was being buried alive.

"Aaaahhhh!" he screeched when he saw the cell. "No, no, no, no! Nooooo! Nooooo!"

The skeletal guards didn't have an answer: they had no tongues or lips, or voice boxes or lungs. Pretty much all of the things you need to speak were missing.

"Noooo! I can't . . . you can't. . . ."

Oh, but they could. And they did. They threw Mack into the cell, pushing his head down with clawlike hands so that he would fit through the short door.

Mack turned and ran at them. He gibbered madly in Vargran, but casting two earlier spells had pretty well wiped out his *enlightened puissance* for now. So he might as well have been speaking Portuguese.[12]

The iron door slammed in his face.

The oil lamp guttered, and for a frozen moment of terror, Mack thought it might go out, and if there's anything worse than being buried alive, it's being buried alive in the dark.

"No! No, you have to let me out! Nooooo!"

One is tempted to look away. Because to keep looking at Mack is to watch him completely fall apart. It's to see our hero whimpering, crying, sobbing, begging for his mother.

You see, a phobia isn't just a fear, like maybe you're afraid you'll fail a test. A phobia is much, much deeper. A phobia taps into the bottommost layers of your brain, down where the brain is just the sediment of evolution and where blunt animal terror lies, far away from your reason and your logic and your calm, soothing voices.

So the Mack we would see in that terrible cell is not the Mack who stood up to Stefan back when Stefan

---

12 A language so difficult even the Portuguese don't speak it.

was the most feared bully at Richard Gere Middle School. (Go, Fighting Pupfish!) Nor would it be the Mack who threw down with Risky in the Australian Outback and killed her once. It's not the Mack who faced dragons and fought Skirrit and treasonous Tong Elves and insane Norse gods and Paddy "Nine Iron" Trout.

It's possible to be very brave some of the time. And pants-wetting scared another time. That's the reality of it. The same person can run away in blind terror one moment, then turn suddenly and face certain death with unearthly determination.

Humans are strange that way.

The thing about Mack's fear was that it was so intense that if you'd told him he was just hours away from being catapulted to certain death, he wouldn't have been even 1 percent more terrified. He had already turned the fear meter up to eleven.

Eight

Jarrah, Dietmar, Xiao, and Stefan were ushered unceremoniously through the door of MacGuffin's castle. The door slammed behind them.

Stefan was back in the enchantment zone and could no longer see the stones and tufts of grass around him, or the castle door closed behind him, or the walls looming above him.

"We have to get him out of there," Stefan said.

"Can't even call me mum for a few good words of Vargran," Jarrah said. "MacGuffin took our phones. What can we do?"

"I . . . ," Dietmar began. Then he shrugged. "I don't know what to do."

Mack would have been secretly pleased to hear that, if he'd been there.

One by one they looked at Xiao. Jarrah said what they were all thinking. "You could fly us over the walls."

Xiao looked down, deep in thought for so long it seemed as if she might have fallen asleep. "I cannot," she said finally in a very sad whisper, and with a slow shake of her head. "There is a treaty. No eastern dragon may appear in the west. To violate the treaty is to risk a war."

"So risk it," Stefan snapped.

Xiao's eyes flashed. "You don't understand: it's not only a risk to dragon folk; if the western dragons were to rise again, entire cities would burn!"

"I don't care," Stefan snarled. He stabbed a finger in the general direction of the door he couldn't see. "He's under my wing. I protect him, and I don't care what gets in my way. He's under my wing!" He raged back and forth, demanding someone show him a rock so he could bang the door down with it.

"If we could find the fairies . . . ," Dietmar said.

"Frank and the others. Connie has betrayed them. They might be able to help us."

"But where are they?" Jarrah shouted. She had caught some of Stefan's wild rage. "Where are the lying little—"

Xiao said, "Wait."

"Wait? Wait on what? Until dawn, when he kills Mack?"

"The fairies cast a Vargran spell that allowed us to see the castle," Xiao said patiently.

"Yes, but only because we have the *enlightened puissance*," Dietmar observed.

Xiao nodded. "The reason there must be twelve of us is that our power grows with each new member of the Magnificent Twelve. True?"

Dietmar snapped his fingers. "Ah! But even if we are only three Magnifica, it may be that our power is greater than the fairies'!"

"We must descend the hill," Xiao said. "And when dawn comes, we must cast the spell and reveal the castle to as many people as we can get together. MacGuffin needs to remain hidden because he is no match for the terrible powers of the modern world. He has his band of skeletons and his spells. But what are these when weighed against the police and the army, and the city planners and zoning officials, the bureaucrats from Brussels, and, worst of all, the tourists who will descend like a plague of locusts should this castle suddenly be revealed to one and all?"

"We will need to practice the spell, doing it together," Dietmar said. "And we will need a good crowd of people to be at the bottom of this hill when morning comes."

"I'll get you a crowd," Stefan said, and everyone believed him.

Oscur exelmo oo-ma!

That was the spell Frank had spoken to reveal the castle. "Hidden castle show! Or else!"

Vargran was a magical language, but not a beautiful one. It got the job done but it wasn't a language for composing song lyrics. And it was dangerous in the hands of one who possessed the *enlightened puissance,* so you could get into a lot of trouble if you didn't get it just right.

But they had all heard the spell quite clearly and they were confident they had the words right. The problem was that, when they thought about it, there wasn't really any way to practice it. Once you used a particular spell, it was a while before you could do it again. And if they sat around testing it out, they might be totally depleted when they needed it.

So instead they practiced saying other things together. They recited the words to Lady Gaga songs. They recited bits of poetry and sang the birthday song in unison, and Jarrah taught them Australian limericks best not repeated here.

Stefan had built a small fire in the rocks at the base of the hill, and the three Magnifica sat around it like a tiny glee club working on their harmony.

"I don't think it will be enough to speak in unison," Xiao said somewhere around four in the morning, with the black sky just beginning to turn navy and the stars just fading the tiniest bit. "We must find a way to unite our hearts, so that our powers will be truly unified."

"I'll unify your hearts," Stefan muttered threateningly. He was getting very tired of standing by helplessly while the three of them sang songs around a campfire.

"Go and focus on how you will get people to this place," Dietmar said, "and stop pacing around here interrupting us."

Jarrah knew immediately that this was a mistake. Dietmar knew it a split second later when he was lifted clear up off the ground and held in the air by his throat. Stefan did this with one hand. He did it without grunting or straining, as if Dietmar were no bigger than a kitten.

"Mack is under my wing," Stefan said. "You . . . are not."

"Stefan is not our servant," Jarrah said sharply.

"Her, I like," Stefan explained further, pointing at Jarrah. "Because she's cool. And her?" Stefan asked, jerking his head toward Xiao. "I told her father I'd take care of her."

"A large, large guy, Xiao's father," Jarrah said. "Large and scary."

"He's not the least bit scary, he's a scholar," Xiao said. "Though," she admitted, "he is large."

Xiao's father was a dragon roughly the size of an entire subway train.

"Put me down," Dietmar said. Then when he

found it suddenly hard to breathe, he added, "Please."

Jarrah gave Stefan a shrug, and he put Dietmar down.

Dietmar rearranged his shirt and smoothed back his hair. "I know that I am not popular. I am never popular," Dietmar said. "Sometimes I seem rude. Because sometimes I am rude. But it is not how I mean to be. I just want to do the correct thing."

Xiao said, "Sometimes people think that I think I am superior. That, too, is not how I feel."

"And people think I'm crazy," Jarrah admitted. "You know, reckless and dangerous." She shrugged. "Well, I am, a bit. But I'm normal otherwise."

"We are all strange creatures," Dietmar said. "I have always known I was to be part of something important. For a long time I did not know what."

"The way I understand it," Stefan said, "it's all or nothing. It takes twelve. All twelve. So you're all in this together."

One by one they nodded.

"So we can't lose anyone. Not even the pipsqueak here."

Dietmar frowned. "What does he mean, pipsqueak?"

"Get your spells or whatever ready," Stefan said. "I'll bring you some witnesses."

With that, he strode off manfully in the direction of the road.

"He is a bully," Dietmar observed.

"Mack says he's the greatest of all bullies," Jarrah said. "Let's get ready. The sun will be coming up soon."

"How do you suppose Mack is faring?" Xiao wondered aloud.

"I'm sure he is fine," Dietmar said.

"He's brave," Xiao said.

"Yeah, the boy will be all right," Jarrah said.

None of them really believed it.

And with good reason, because at that very moment Mack was huddled in a corner of his tiny cell, pulling himself into as small a space as he could, as if that would make the rest of the cell seem larger. Less coffin-like.

He stared mostly at the skull lamp. It was just about the only thing there was to stare at. The alternative was staring at the chamber pot. That wasn't a great alternative, although the porcelain did have a pleasant blue flower pattern. And the firelight did reflect like a second small flame from the shiny . . .

Hold up.

There was something other than firelight reflected in the chamber pot. Mack badly needed something to take his attention off the whole buried-alive thing so he conducted a small experiment: he moved his hands to block the skull light from reaching the chamber pot.

Sure enough, there was an entirely different glow in the porcelain. It was a whiter light.

Mack scrambled forward on hands and knees and stuck his face right close to the pot. Not a good choice if you were looking for a pleasant smell. But, as it happened, useful in a way that made Mack's heart leap. For there in the porcelain was the tiny, dim image of Grimluk.

"Grimluk!"

"Is that you, Mack of the Magnifica?"

"Of course it's me!"

"Can you turn up the lights? It seems awfully dark where you are. And my time is short . . . my power . . . fades. . . ."

"Whoa! No no no. None of that power-fading baloney! I'm in a dungeon!"

Grimluk was one of the original Magnificent

Twelve. He was no longer 12, of course; in fact he was 3,012. How he had managed to cling to life for better than three thousand years, Mack did not know. Nor did he know where Grimluk was. Presumably some distant cave. Or possibly a secret compound. Although it occurred to Mack that, for all he knew, Grimluk might be sitting by the pool at the Beverly Hills Hotel drinking mojitos.

In which case Mack really hated him, because he would have loved to be there with Grimluk.

Though not if Grimluk was wearing a bathing suit. Grimluk was 3,012 years old, after all, and had a beard that was rated "three Civil War generals" in size and bushiness. He had eyebrows that would have had Dumbledore reaching for the scissors. He was so wrinkled you could stash french fries down in some of the folds of skin.[13]

All this, though, was beside the point. The real point was that it was Grimluk who had first informed Mack that he was required to assemble a group of twelve twelve-year-olds possessed of the *enlightened puissance.*

Or to put it another way: it was all Grimluk's fault.

---

13 No, no idea why you would want to.

"Where have you been?" Mack demanded furiously. "I haven't heard from you in a long time."

"This apparition thing isn't easy," Grimluk protested. "I'm old. I'm weak. I'm not the man I once was. I fail, I—"

"Get me out of here!" Mack cried. He grabbed the chamber pot and held it close so that he could look Grimluk in the eye. "Listen to me: some crazy person has me in a dungeon and he's going to kill me."

"Who?"

"Me!"

"No, Mack of the Magnifica, I mean, who is holding you?"

"William Blisterthöng MacGuffin!"

"Ouch," Grimluk said, and bit his lip and shook his head and just generally did not look encouraging. "No lotion ever created by man or magic really deals with the symptoms of blisterthong. I had a case back in, oh, I guess it would have been the year—"

"Grimluk! Focus! I have to escape!"

"Have you tried—"

And there the image of Grimluk faded out, leaving Mack staring at the chamber pot.

"No! No! Get back here!"

He was still yelling at the porcelain when he heard the bolt on the door thrown back. He dropped the pot, spun, and leaped for the opening, fast as a tiger.

A skeletal hand closed over his arm and pulled him out into the passageway. Unfortunately two more skeletons were at the ready and grabbed him.

Mack tried his best to think of a Vargran spell. He was seriously cursing his own laziness—he really should have studied—and running through the Vargran he'd used in the past.

The obvious one was the spell he'd used to burn up Risky.

That one he remembered.

Oh, he remembered it just fine.

E-ma edras.

If he could burn Risky, he could surely burn MacGuffin.

Nine

MEANWHILE, AT RICHARD GERE MIDDLE SCHOOL[14]

"**M**r. MacAvoy. Are you . . . are you . . . ? Never mind."

That was Mack's English teacher, Ms. Telford. Ms. Telford had asked the golem—who she believed to be Mack, of course—numerous questions over the last week, and she had never liked the answers much.

---

14 Actually, the Fighting Pupfish are 0 and 78. But *Go, Fighting Pupfish!* anyway.

She had, for example, once asked the golem whether he could please speak up in answer to a question. The golem had said, "Up!" Which might be a perfectly understandable error to make. But she had then said, "I meant could you speak a little louder. Project your voice, Mr. MacAvoy."

The golem had projected his voice. He said, "UP!" very loudly. And he projected his voice onto a silk plant that sat forlornly on the edge of Ms. Telford's desk.

And then he projected his voice onto the flag, and onto the shelf of ancient books so that it seemed exactly as if some old copies of Animorphs books were yelling, "UP! UP! UP!"

And then the backpacks beside each desk began yelling it, one after the next, while kids jumped up shouting, "How did you do that?"

It had been extremely upsetting.

Ms. Telford had learned that if she wasn't absolutely, 100 percent sure of the answer she'd get, it was best not to ask Mack any questions.

So she stopped herself.

But Matthew Morgan—nerd bully—was sitting behind the golem and decided to poke the golem in the back and say, "You're getting fat, MacAvoy."

"No, I'm getting big," the golem responded.

And sure enough, he was getting big.

"I'm a big boy," the golem said proudly. And he stood up. Which unfortunately caused his desk to get up with him because he was now wedged tightly into it, so tightly that it was hard to see how he was ever going to get out of it.

Matthew stood up slowly, his face a mask of dawning horror. He stood up to his full height, and there was no denying that the golem was taller. Taller by a good foot. And broader by another foot.

"Is this big?" the golem asked.

At his biggest and scariest, Stefan Marr had never been this big. The golem looked like a pale, pleasant-faced Incredible Hulk. Only maybe not so much Incredible as Unusual. Or Odd. The Odd Hulk.

Because while he had grown taller and broader, and he absolutely filled out his shoes, jeans, and shirt, he had not ripped any seams but rather had expanded in all the parts that were beyond his confining clothing.

His ankles were huge.

His forearms looked like Popeye's—postspinach.

His neck was the size of a tree trunk.

And his head was a watermelon. Figuratively speaking.

In Ms. Telford's class every jaw hung open. Every eye bulged. But Matthew wasn't just amazed, he was threatened.

"Been working out, huh?" he demanded. And he sort of turned his head back and forth in a tough-guy way that made his neck crack. And then he laced his fingers together and cracked his knuckles the way he'd seen Stefan do. And then he hunched his shoulders and tried to swell his pecs and biceps and whatever the other muscles are called.

Then, as he gazed at the golem's massive, Thanksgiving-turkey-sized forearms, something seemed to die behind the bully's eyes.

He sat down.

Ms. Telford had a strange, faraway look in her eyes. The golem thought it might be a look of admiration. Actually it was Ms. Telford imagining the margarita with extra salt that would be waiting for her when she left school at the end of the day.

Ms. Telford often pictured that margarita.

"Mr. MacAvoy, you need to go see the principal," she said regretfully.

"Do you want me to tell him something?" the golem asked helpfully.

"No. I think he'll figure it out all on his own."

The golem turned toward the door. He felt as if he had perhaps done something wrong and didn't quite understand what it was.

So he was feeling a little self-conscious as he headed down the lonely hallway, banging the edge of his desk against the lockers as he walked.

Camaro was seated in a chair outside her own class.

"Hey, Mack," she said. "What are you doing?"

"Going to see the principal. Why are you sitting in the hallway?"

She shrugged. "Kicked me out for not knowing an answer."

"What was the question?"

She made a grin that didn't last very long. "Teacher asked me what my problem was. I didn't have an answer."

"Why did she ask you that?"

Camaro waved her hand dismissively. "I superglued

the chalk to the board. It was kind of cool, I thought. Five pieces. They were the points of a star if you looked at it the right way. I thought . . ." She glanced up at him, self-conscious. Then she forced a laugh. "I thought it was kind of artistic."

"I wish I had seen it," the golem said.

"They're in there chiseling it off now," Camaro said. And indeed the golem heard the sound of a hammer striking a steel chisel. "I'll see you tomorrow, right? For the fight?"

"Yes. They can punch me if they want. It doesn't bother me. Especially now that I'm big."

"Watch your head, by the way. You could bump into that doorjamb."

Ten

The skeletal crew threw Mack onto the ground before the throne of William Blisterthöng MacGuffin. The landing skinned Mack's knees. Not that this was his major concern right then, but it was still painful.

His hands were bound behind him, but his feet were free and he had a plan.

"Ah heard a lot o' screaming frae yer cell. Some weeping tae," MacGuffin said. He grinned his yellow-toothed grin inside his bristly red beard-of-fear. "Sae ye'r a feartie-cat. A weeping, blubbering wee feartie-cat."

"I am not a feartie-cat," Mack said. "I'm phobic."

That stopped the conversation for a few seconds while Connie, who was fluttering around MacGuffin like a tween around Justin Bieber, explained to MacGuffin.

MacGuffin looked different in daylight. He still had the exploding head-bush of red hair; and the sallow, wrinkly skin; and the too-large teeth, but now he seemed almost to sparkle a bit around the edges. Like someone had sprinkled him with glitter.

Ah, Mack thought: fairy dust. That would make sense.

He took a step toward MacGuffin. "See? I'm not afraid of you."

Well, of course he was. Because as you know, among Mack's numerous phobias was an irrational fear of beards. He was fine with beards at a distance. But a beard up close caused him acute feelings of panic.

He'd once had a horrible dream in which he'd been locked in a room full of rabbis, imams, and Santa Clauses. In his dream he had searched frantically through Santa's bag, looking for a razor. All he had found were socks.

The mere memory of that dream gave him the shakes.

Mack had a beard comfort zone of about ten feet. A beard farther away than that just made him vaguely nauseous. A beard at, say, eight feet would make him start to feel the first slight edge of panic. And a beard within three feet would have him sweating, weeping, and begging an unfeeling heaven for an angel-barber armed with clippers to save him.

MacGuffin unfortunately had the worst of all possible beards: wild and red. So subtract a foot from each of those distances.

At a distance of five feet, Mack wasn't sure he could incinerate MacGuffin. At the same time, he wasn't sure he could force himself to move any closer.

Somewhere there was a math formula that balanced "likelihood of incineration" against "fear of beards," but Mack didn't know it. He had probably been daydreaming in that class.

"You should be afraid," Connie said, and made an expressive hand gesture that was a pantomime of throat cutting. "You should be very afraid."

Mack needed to get closer to use the Vargran spell. He wished that Connie would get out of the way because he figured she was just blinded by love, and he didn't need to burn her up.

MacGuffin, on the other hand, had it coming.

Now out of the coffin-cell, out in the air with a blue sky overhead and a cool breeze on his face, Mack was recovering fast from his night of terror but now edging into full-blown beard panic.

But here's the thing about Mack: he was scared of many things, but he wasn't weak. He could hold it together. Usually.

Except for times when he couldn't.

"Where are my friends?" Mack demanded, and took another bold step forward.

MacGuffin shot a conspiratorial look at Connie. The two of them seemed to share a private laugh.

"You don't need to worry about your friends," Connie said. "In a few minutes you won't need to worry about anything at all. Ever again."

Another step closer. Four feet from a bushy red beard!

Close enough. And now Mack decided it was too bad about Connie, but she was a bad, bad fairy. And if Mack died here, all of humanity was doomed.

"Fur th' crime o' invading mah secret hame 'n' trying tae steal mah possessions, ah sentence ye tae death, Mack o' th' Magnifica!" MacGuffin cried, and pounded his stick on the ground.

"Oh yeah?" Mack snarled. "And I sentence you to fry like a hamburger." With a supreme effort of courage he closed his eyes and leaped toward MacGuffin and his beard and cried, "*E-ma edras!*"

The light was like an explosion. Like someone had taken all the light of the sun, squeezed it into a balloon, then popped that balloon.

It was like a small nuclear fireball.

The heat instantly incinerated two skeletal guards.

It scorched the very walls and made the mortar bubble from between the seams of the stones.

MacGuffin and Connie wavered, like reflections in troubled water.

But not like they were burning up.

The light faded. The searing heat, which had spared Mack as the one who had cast the spell, dissipated.

And MacGuffin still sat calmly while Connie floated on gossamer wings.

"Um . . . ," Mack said. "Why . . . why aren't you . . ."

"Dead?" MacGuffin asked, and burst out laughing. "Whit a stoatin' gowk A'd be tae let ye wirk a Vargran spell oan me."

Which in English was, "What am I, a moron?"

"Turn around, you foolish child," Connie said.

Slowly Mack turned.

There at the far end of the courtyard was the throne, and MacGuffin upon it. The appearance—the illusion—of MacGuffin just a few feet away from Mack faded like the last scene of a movie.

"'Tis nae enough tae huv th' power, ye mist huv th' cunning tae uise it."

Or: "It's not enough to have the power, you must have the cunning to use it."

A half dozen skeletons of various species came at a rush.

"You've used up your *enlightened puissance* for a while," Connie said. "And by the time you are strong enough to cast another Vargran spell . . . well . . ."

And that is how we come to the point where Mack

was bound in the basket of a trebuchet.

"Cheerio the nou, ye scunner," MacGuffin said, and he swung the sword.

The blade parted the frayed rope.

Gravity worked the way it usually does, and the big basket of rocks dropped like a big basket of rocks.

"Aaaahhh!" Mack screamed.

It was like being shot from a cannon.

Mack flew like . . . okay, like a cannonball.

The flight lasted only seconds. Then he hit the wall of Urquhart Castle. His bones were all broken. His skull popped open like a dropped melon. He was dead before the gelatinous mass of his pulverized body could ooze down to—

Okay, that's not what happened. It's what would have happened. Except that Stefan had made good on his promise to round up a crowd.

He had done it by spotting a pair of tour buses that were parked just off the road at Urquhart Castle, waiting to visit said castle and watch the sun rise and light up Loch Ness.

Stefan banged on the doors and then each of the windows of the buses, hammering them with his fists and yelling, "The Loch Ness monster is running around loose! Grab your cameras!"

For a while the sleepy tourists just stared at him. Then, one man—a man with two cameras slung around his neck—broke and ran for the door.

"This way!" Stefan shouted, and the man, bless his gullible heart, followed.

Well, that was all it took. Because there was no way the rest of the tourists were going to sit idly by while that one guy got all the good pictures.

In a flash both buses were gushing forth the usual bus-tourist folk: people in Bermuda shorts who had no business wearing shorts; old couples with matching plaid outfits; sullen goth teenagers who couldn't believe they were stuck touring with their grandparents OMG; guys with unfortunate facial hair; women in giant bonnets; the kind of old dudes who like to repeat stupid jokes until you laugh just to make them stop; cheek pinchers; sour-faced crones; tiny Asian people who take pictures of everything, even the bus tires; vegans wearing hemp T-shirts—the entire cross section of subspecies *Touristus fotograficus*.[15]

All of them raced after Stefan, who led them away

---

15 Yes, that's absolutely a real thing, Google it if you don't— Okay, don't Google it; I made it up.

from the actual lake and toward a hill that neither they (nor Stefan himself) could see.

The crowd faltered then.

They slowed.

They began to think they were being made fools of. Then Jarrah, Xiao, and Dietmar rose from behind a stone wall.

The three of them joined hands. They focused on what united them: affection and concern for Mack, a Determination[16] to Stop the Pale Queen, and Regret[17] at not getting some Magnum bars for themselves.

Hands linked, with Jarrah in the middle.

Hands linked, they climbed atop the stone wall. And for the first time in 3,000 years, a group spell was spoken in the Vargran language.

"Oscur exelmo oo-ma!"

The three Magnifica waited. Tense. Scared.

And then, the goth tourist kid said, "Whoa."

She was a girl. Not quite a teen. Maybe . . . well, exactly . . . twelve years old.

"There's a castle there. On top of a mountain."

She was with her grandparents. Not the wrinkled-up

---

16 With a capital *D*.

17 With a capital *R*.

type of grandparents—these were the active, fit, nutrition-beverage-drinking kind of grandparents.

And they saw it, too.

Not all the tourists did. But some did. At least half of those standing there were looking up with their jaws down and their eyes wide and their cameras forgotten for a moment.

"What are you all staring at?" others demanded, frustrated.

One of the bus drivers said, "I've lived here all my life: I've never seen this. It's . . . it's impossible."

"No, not impossible," Dietmar announced somewhat grandly. "It is the castle of William Blisterthöng MacGuffin, long concealed by fairy magic."

The crowd continued the jaws-hanging, eyes-wide thing, but now some were pointing their cameras and others were moving toward the castle.

A scream pierced the air.

A cannonball flew from the castle's highest tower.

The cannonball was writhing and yelling.

Xiao, Jarrah, and Dietmar all saw it at the same instant.

Stefan cried out in anguished recognition.

No chance to use Vargran! The three Magnifica

had used up their *enlightened puissance* revealing the castle.

"Noooo!" Xiao cried.

Mack flew in a long, flat arc straight toward the unyielding stone walls of Urquhart Castle.

"Halk-ma simu (ch)ias!"

The Vargran spell rang out clear and loud.

And it came from the goth girl, who stood legs apart, both hands together, and pointing with her clenched fist, like she was aiming a gun or something, as Mack flew overhead.

Eleven

What do you think about in the seconds before death?

Have you ever considered that? You're probably considering it right now.

In Mack's case he was thinking about his life. Which, prior to Grimluk suddenly informing him of his importance in an age-old struggle between good and evil, had been pretty boring.

And Mack was thinking about how great boring is. Boring is excellent, compared to dying.

In those last seconds he was thinking about his mom. And screaming. And his dad. And screaming.

And he was feeling guilty because now the world would not be saved and the Pale Queen would enslave all of humanity. She would probably outlaw video games and movies and fro-yo and Toaster Strudel and all the truly good things in the world.

And then there was the screaming.

And suddenly Mack heard a voice, audible even over the shriek of the wind whipping past.

He didn't think he recognized the voice. Then again, it's sometimes hard to recognize voices when you're screaming and hurtling to your death.

"Halk-ma simu (ch)ias!"

The walls of Urquhart Castle were so close that Mack could see ants crawling up the rock when all of a sudden he was free of the rope and his arms spread and caught the wind.

The wind filled his wings and he soared!

His what now?

His wings!

It strained very muscle fiber in his body. It was like he was being stretched on a rack, but his wings took the wind, filled, shot him up, up, up past the wall, so close that the tip of his nose scraped the rock, and then he was up over the walls, up in the air, zooming up into the sky.

Up and up until momentum died away and he sort of hung there between acceleration and gravity.

Gravity gently tugged at him, and he began to fall. But his wings—they were like a seagull's wings, actually, white and swept back, but as wide in span as the largest condor's—held him aloft.

His feet were melted together and had sprouted a wide fan of feathers. The rest of him was pretty much regular old Mack.

He caught an updraft and swooped low above a crowd of utterly amazed faces, all turned skyward.

He would have liked to land, but no feet.

So he hovered in the sky, riding the thermal,[18] floating on an updraft of warm air rippling up from the grassy field.

A girl with black lipstick dressed in black, white, and a few strategic accents of red, looked up at him and said, "Say, '*Halk-ma simu (ch)ias!*'"

So because she seemed to know what was going on,

---

18 Thermals are strong updrafts of warm air, and birds ride them like elevators. Seriously.

Mack said, "*Halk-ma simu (ch)ias!*"

And with that his wings folded in on themselves. And the feathered tail split again into legs.

Unfortunately he was still about twenty feet in the air, so he dropped like a stone.

Stefan leaped and caught him before he hit the ground.

"Dude," Stefan said, and set Mack on his feet.

Mack's legs felt like they might buckle. He had had a pretty bad twenty-four hours, really, and shakiness was natural.

"Thanks," Mack said to Stefan.

"You're alive," Jarrah said with a satisfied grin. "Was it kind of cool?"

His friends rushed to embrace him. Even Dietmar. And after some backslapping and whatnot, Mack disengaged and went to the goth girl.

"You saved my life," he said.

"*Oui*," she said. Which is French for "yeah."

"You're one of us," he said.

"Yes, I am."

"What's your name?"

"Sylvie Zola de Rochefort," she said. It was a lot of

name for a girl who wasn't very big. She was definitely smaller than Jarrah and even smaller than Xiao.

Her black hair was cut to chin length. Her eyes were dark and somewhat sad-looking. Her lashes were absurdly long and curved up to add a quizzical air to the sadness. Her skin was naturally pale—she didn't seem to be wearing goth or emo white makeup. But her lipstick was black and her fingernails were bloodred.

"My name is Mack. This is Jarrah, Xiao, Dietmar, and my friend and bodyguard, Stefan."

"Good catch, friend and bodyguard," Sylvie said to Stefan.

"Huh," Stefan replied.

"Where are you from, Sylvie?" Mack asked.

"A tiny little town in France, called Fouras. It is nowhere special."

She pronounced *special* as *spess-ee-al*. Mack liked that. He liked it a lot.

"Okay, life stories later. Right now we need to go get that Key from MacGuffin," Mack said. (Give the boy credit: he recovered quickly.) "Who are all these people?"

"Tourists," Xiao said.

"They can see the castle?"

"Most of them appear to be aware of the castle," Dietmar said.

"Okay, then," Mack said. Then he raised his voice to be heard by all. You might wonder why a bunch of tourists would listen to Mack. After all, he was just a kid. But it's a fact: if you want to get people's attention, being catapulted through the air and then turning into a sort of goofy bird is a pretty good way to do it.

"Listen to me," Mack said. "No one has seen that castle in a thousand years. A thousand years! Plus there are walking skeletons in there. Can you imagine the YouTube possibilities? The person who gets the best video online will get millions of hits. Millions!"

"And don't forget Facebook, Google Plus, and Twitter," Jarrah pointed out.

"You'll be more important in the Twitterverse than Ashton Kutcher," Mack said.

After that, nothing was going to stop the horde. Roughly sixty-five people and approximately a hundred cameras began to march to the castle.

The rough climb over the rocks thinned the herd a bit, but in the end the Magnificent Five were accompanied to MacGuffin's gate by about forty hardy men and women.

"William Blisterthöng MacGuffin!" Mack yelled at the closed door. "You have visitors!"

There was a long silence. Then, "Go away!"

"No," Mack said.

Another long silence. Then, "Gang awa', ye interlopers. Ah demand mah privacy. Ah huv rights!"

"You lost your rights when you tried to kill me!" Mack shouted back.

Stefan used a big rock to bang on the door. *BANG BANG BANG.*

"Stop banging, ye'll ruin mah door. That's hert o' oak, ye cannae buy wood lik' that anymair!"

MacGuffin was concerned about the woodwork.

"Then open the door and give me the Key!" Mack yelled. "And our phones!"

This time the silence dragged on and on. But Mack made a "stay put" gesture at his posse and they waited.

Then, with a clattering of chains and locks, the door opened a crack. Bristly beard and a single eye came into view. Every camera was rolling.

MacGuffin thrust out a hairy hand holding a stone

circle perhaps seven inches across, with a hole in the middle.

Mack did not want to get near enough to that beard to take the stone. He nodded at Stefan, who stepped forward.

"Grrrr," MacGuffin said furiously at Stefan.

"Grrrr back at you," Stefan snarled.

"The phones," Mack said, his voice hard.

A fairy hand pushed a burlap bag out of the door, then withdrew.

The door slammed shut.

Mack turned to the somewhat disappointed tourists. "Listen, folks: we've got what we came for. We have to go. But you can all stay and drive that guy crazy."

No one likes a spoiler, but no one likes a story that skips over an interesting development, either. Mack and the Magnifica have to move on. But just so you know: within a few days MacGuffin had cracked and opened his castle for regular tours. In fact, he was making a pretty penny from a gift shop that featured William Blisterthöng MacGuffin dolls and a recording of MacGuffin's craziest rants.

Connie appeared in the background of a YouTube video but was never seen by the public. The rumor is that she moved to Ireland to avoid Frank's revenge.

As for Mack, he would be going to France. Why? Because Sylvie said, "There are two others like us, Mack. They are hiding in Paris. I risked everything to join you so that you and your friends might save them."

"Save them from what?" Mack asked.

"They have all come to Paris, Mack, all the forces of evil. They knew there were three of us who had gathered there, so they came to Paris to kill us and leave you powerless to complete the Twelve."

"When you say, 'They have all,' what do you mean by that?"

"The Tong Elves. Bowands. Skirrit. They say there is even a Gudridan—a giant—and maybe more. All under the command of two people: the man in green and his apprentice—he who is the twelfth of us."

"Valin?"

"Yes," Sylvie said. "My half brother, Valin, the twelfth of the Twelve."

Twelve

Sylvie had a short and emotionally repressed parting from her grandparents, who apparently understood that she would have to be gone for a while saving the world. There were shrugs, a few small hand gestures, and they did the kiss-kiss-on-the-cheeks thing.

The now–Magnificent Five plus Stefan crammed back into the car and drove with their usual destructiveness—two sideswiped cars, a crushed stop sign, and a young woman on a bike who had to plow into a ditch to escape injury[19]—to reach the Clansman Hotel, where a boat could be found to take them out onto Loch Ness itself.

Normally the boat would take a whole load of tourists, but the tourists were all still busy at Castle Blisterthöng—as it would come to be known—so Mack and his friends had the boat to themselves.

The captain was extremely reluctant to allow them to stop in the middle of the loch and use his megaphone to begin shouting at the water. But, as you may recall, Mack had a million-dollar credit card and, again, it's kind of amazing what you can get people to do when you have that much money.

Boat rental: 500 GBP.[20]

So the boat, HMS *Heather Lochlear*, stopped and wallowed in the midst of Loch Ness. It's a fairly narrow lake—you can see both sides at once—but quite long, so you can't see end to end. They could see Urquhart Castle quite clearly and Blisterthöng Castle beyond—a sight that had the captain losing his meerschaum pipe into the water when his jaw dropped in amazement.

---

19 Also, the Magnificent Five would like to extend their apologies to the cow.
20 Yes, that's kind of a lot in real money.

He had a bit of the *enlightened puissance*, the captain had. After all, you don't spend your life floating around and looking for the Loch Ness monster without possessing a powerful imagination.

After seeing the castle that had never been there before, the captain was very cooperative.

Mack had no clear idea how to let the All-Mother, aka the Loch Ness monster, know that he had the two pieces of the Vargran Key in his possession and was now ready to free her from the curse that had been placed on her.

If you think about it, talking to a sea serpent whose very existence is in doubt is not an easy proposition.

So he borrowed the captain's megaphone, climbed out onto the very tip of the bow, and yelled, "All-Mother. I have what you need!"

When that didn't work, he yelled, "Frank the fairy sent me!"

Which also didn't work.

"Her names," Dietmar said. "Frank told us her names. Maybe they have the power to summon her."

"Does anyone remember the names?" Mack asked.

Dietmar raised his hand.

"Anyone besides Dietmar?" Mack asked.

The rest all looked down at the ground.

"Okay, Dietmar," Mack said. He handed the megaphone to the blond boy and let him take his place in the bow.

"Eimhur Ceana Una Mordag!" Dietmar cried.

Nothing.

"And All-Mother to clan Begonia," Dietmar added.

Still nothing. Just faint ripples from the chill breeze that blew across the surface of the water.

"Beloved of the Gods and Ultimate Warrioress?" Dietmar tried, obviously beginning to doubt his plan now.

Still nothing.

"But that was all," Dietmar said, shrugging his shoulders and looking perplexed.

"No, there was one more thing," Xiao said. "I remember! Holder of the record for longest sustained note on the bagpipes!"

"But that is silly," Dietmar protested.

"Try it," Mack said.

So Dietmar pressed the button on the megaphone and said, "Eimhur Ceana Una Mordag, All-Mother to clan Begonia, Beloved of the Gods, Ultimate Warrioress, and a past holder of the record for longest sustained note on the bagpipes, please speak with us!"

"Thar she blows!" the captain cried. Not exactly in those words, because that's from *Moby-Dick*. What the captain actually said does not bear repeating and should never have been said in front of a bunch of twelve-year-olds. But you have to understand: the man was excited. He had navigated these waters for thirty-two years and never even caught a glimpse of Nessie.

The captain was the first to see—but then Mack did as well—the bulge of water, a moving wave. It was as though a submarine were powering by just beneath the surface.

Then an eruption! A geyser of water, and up and up and up rose something like a snake. A very big snake, but not with a snake's head. No, the head was more distinct, more elongated, more like something that ought to be attached to a dinosaur.

The head was the size of the car they'd been driving. The mouth had a bit of a quirky dolphin smile about it, and the eyes were intelligent and alert.

Nessie's body surfaced only partially, like a whale.

There were fins, four of them, that lay on the surface of the water acting as stabilizers. A long tail, almost as long as the elevated neck, swished back and forth like the tail of an agitated cat.

Nessie could train only one eye at a time on them. She chose to aim her left eye at them.

"You have summoned me," a voice said, but the voice did not seem to come from that massive dinosaur head. Nor was it the sort of voice you would associate with a giant sea serpent. It sounded like the voice of a woman, perhaps a bit haughty, maybe a little proud, a little sure of herself, with maybe just a bit of Queen Elizabeth II falsetto in there.

"Well, yes," Mack admitted. "We summoned you."

The head lowered and the eye peered hard at Xiao. "What is your kind doing here, dragon?"

"I am here as a girl," Xiao said, and made an open-arms gesture of "I'm harmless" and "so please don't kill me."

Nessie—the All-Mother of clan Begonia—did not seem happy about the presence of a Chinese dragon, however much she disguised herself as a girl. In fact Nessie looked very much as if she might be really annoyed. So Mack moved quickly in front of Xiao and said, "We were sent by Frank. We have the Key."

Nessie stopped caring about Xiao in a heartbeat. "You have the Key of William Blisterthöng MacGuffin?"

"That's right," Mack said. "Totally."

He drew out the smaller center piece from his pocket.

The All-Mother's eye glittered.

Then he pulled out the second part, heavier, rather awkward, from where he had slipped it into the waist of his pants.

"The Key!" the sea serpent hissed.

"The deal with Frank was that if he helped us get it, we'd use it to free you," Mack explained.

"And then, with the Key in my possession, I can have my revenge!" Nessie exulted. "My foes will flee before me! I will crush all other fairy clans! I will rain down fire on Blisterthöng! I will sink every boat that has ever chased me around this forsaken lake. And then, on to the destruction of towns and villages!"

"Um . . . ," Mack said.

"What happened to fairies being a peaceful

people?" Jarrah asked.

"We aren't giving you the Key," Mack said. "That wasn't the deal."

"Frank is a good fairy," Nessie said. "But he doesn't make decisions like that. I do! Now: give me the Key!"

"No, we can't do that if you're going to go rampaging around and . . . you know. Kill everyone."

Nessie got a crafty look in her sea serpent eye. "You're right; I won't do that."

"I kind of don't believe you," Mack said.

"You can absolutely believe me," Nessie said with utmost sincerity. "I could not be more trustworthy. That other stuff I said? Fairy humor. Ha. Ha-ha. See?"

"Look, all I can do is what I agreed to," Mack said. "I can free you from the spell. But there's no way I'm going to let you have the Key. We need it to defeat the Pale Queen. Plus, you're obviously nuts."

At this she lowered her head until it was level with Mack's. "If the Key were to sink to the bottom of the loch, I would be the only one who could find it."

"Well, I'm not going to drop it into—" And then Mack stopped, because he got where she was going. "Oh."

Up shot the massive dinosaur head.

Then down it came in a rush, water spraying and then surging up, and the head slammed (!) straight down at the deck.

Mack shoved Xiao aside and Stefan tripped backward, accidentally knocking Dietmar out of the way.

The monster's head hit the deck like someone had dropped a safe. The whole boat shook. But the deck was steel so it didn't break.

The same could not be said for the railing, the deck chairs, and the chest where they kept life jackets. These were all bent and splintered.

Rrraaaww-chug-chug-rrraawww!

The captain threw the boat into reverse. The engines responded quickly but not quickly enough. Nessie, the All-Mother of clan Begonia, was quick. She spun around more like a cat than a massive sea serpent and slammed her tail into the side of the boat. There was a loud splintering sound, and Mack, who had just gotten to his feet, was knocked off balance again.

The boat gathered speed, but it was moving backward, which was not its best angle.

Nessie easily kept pace, swimming alongside, her

head high out of the water, then veered into the boat. The boat and the sea serpent were roughly the same size, but Nessie had the speed and the agility. The impact pushed the boat over so that the deck canted sharply and Jarrah went flying, hit the tangled railing, and was barely saved by Stefan's quickly outstretched hand.

He yanked her back aboard. The captain killed the engines—at this angle and moving backward, he was going to poop the boat.

(This requires some explanation. For a boat to be "pooped" means being swamped by a wave coming over the stern. Get your mind out of the gutter.)

That's right: they were seconds away from the boat being pooped.

So the captain killed the engine and turned the rudder hard, trying to use the momentum to spin around forward.

This almost worked. It worked in the sense that Nessie sheered off and the boat wallowed wildly in its own wave. Water rolled over the sides, drenching everyone.

The captain hit the throttle—going forward this time—and the boat began to move slowly.

Nessie was way too quick for that move. She came racing alongside, and before the boat could gather way (get going), she soared up out of the water like a whale showing off, twisted just slightly in the air, and landed directly across the bow.

It was like an elephant dropping from the sky.

Fortunately there was some yielding give in her rubbery flesh because Sylvie and Dietmar were both slammed to the deck, crushed beneath her massive bulk, and only saved from being popped like a couple of stomped hot dogs by the fact that the boat hit a trough and dropped away, lessening the impact.

Nessie slithered off, leaving two kids down, unable to move. And all of a sudden, things had gotten very, very serious. There was blood coming from Dietmar's eyes and nose, gushing and mingling with water on the deck.

Sylvie didn't move at all. She just lay there like she was unconscious. Or something worse.

"That breaks the deal," Mack snarled. "Stefan, Jatrah, get them inside. Xiao: with me. We need to do some fast decoding."

Thirteen

The boat was under way again, but the captain had been injured in the latest attack. He was up on the flying bridge with what might be a broken arm and leg, trying bravely to keep going, but looking like a guy who was likely to pass out cold at any . . . and there he went.

The wheel spun free and the boat veered straight for a rocky shore.

"Stefan!" Mack yelled.

Stefan swung out through a shattered cabin

window and swarmed up to the bridge with the powerful agility of a chimpanzee. Although it would be a bad idea to ever compare him to a chimp to his face.

The boat turned away from shore. Mack fumbled the pieces of the Key together. The center stone fit perfectly.

For the first time he had a chance to really take a look at the two pieces together.

In the very center was a symbol of an eyeball. The eyeball didn't do much but stare at you.

Around the outer edge of the outer ring were a large number of pictures—tiny images carved into the stone. Some were fairly easy to understand. For example, a circle with rays coming out was probably the sun. Three wavy lines probably meant water. A wild boar with puffed-out cheeks was surely wind. Or maybe just a wild boar.

Others were even more obscure. There was the head of an animal that might be a horse but might also be a cow. It wasn't that easy to tell. Mack didn't have time to count, but there were 144 symbols: twelve times twelve.

"They are objects. Nouns," Xiao said, pointing.

Mack had noticed that, too.

The inner circle was a different set of symbols but with some overlap. For example, there was a second puffy-cheeked cloud. There were also really odd symbols like a fist, a held nose, a sign on a stick, what looked like a rabbit in a hat, a foot with wings, a fluttering leaf, a knife, a wheel, and so on.

"Those are verbs," Mack said, rushing to get it out before Xiao could.

"Verbs and nouns. But . . . ," Xiao said.

And that's when Nessie dived under the boat and surfaced beneath it. The entire boat, but especially the bow, rose up out of the water. All the way clear. As in, the bow was pointing roughly at the highest part of Urquhart Castle.

Mack and Xiao slammed back into the front cabin window. Mack held on to the Key for dear life.

Then Nessie rolled beneath the boat and, just as the bow was beginning to plunge, she raised the stern. The *Heather Lochlear* went down like a skipped rock that had had its last skip. Mack was underwater. All the way under.

Freezing, foaming loch was in his clothing and in

125

his nose and ears and smearing his vision. His fingers gripping the Key were instantly numb. And it's funny just how quickly you start to need air when you're underwater and you were caught on the exhale.

Both Mack and Xiao floated free of the deck, which fell away beneath them, farther and farther, and then, right in their faces, there was the monster. Her dolphin grin wasn't looking so quirky now because she opened her jaws and showed row upon row of very white, very sharp teeth.

But then the boat reached the bottom of its plunge and rose, fighting its way back to the surface. The bow caught Nessie right in the neck. Mack heard an underwater bellow of pain, and all at once the bow was bursting up through the silvery barrier between water and air.

Mack gasped for air. His fingers were so numb he couldn't feel the Key, but through dripping eyes he confirmed that both pieces were still in his hands.

Nessie was a hundred feet away, twisting her neck back and forth above the water like an athlete limbering up.

Stefan did what Stefan could be absolutely relied

upon to do. He shoved all throttles forward and aimed the boat for the All-Mother of clan Begonia.

"My turn," Stefan said.

The sudden attack threw Nessie off her game. At first she stared like she couldn't believe it. And in that time the boat closed half the distance.

By the time she realized that yes, yes, they were actually attacking her, she only had time to run. Or swim; let's not get literal here.

"Get some of that encapsulated pissant going!" Stefan yelled down at Mack. "She's faster than the boat!"

Mack and Xiao fumbled with the Key. "I don't know how to use it!" Xiao cried.

"Me neither!"

"Verbs and nouns. What do we do with them? And what about modifiers?" asked Xiao.

"Look!" Mack pointed with one trembling finger. "That's a picture of rocks!"

"So what?"

"And that symbol with two hands making a ball . . . I think that means 'make.'"

"Quick, line them up!"

They did that. And instantly . . . nothing!

"Are we making a rock?"

"I guess not," Mack gibbered.

"Wait, wait. I have it! Okay, first line 'make' up with that monster. Then the rocks. We'll sink her!"

"Say what?" Mack asked.

But together they did it.

And instantly . . . still nothing.

But then, two instants later, there came a voice.

The voice said, "*A-ma belast dafee.*"

"Did you hear that?" Mack asked.

Xiao nodded, or maybe just shivered in a vertical direction, but it looked like a nod and, anyway, Mack had no better plan. Because now, as Stefan had predicted, Nessie had outrun and outmaneuvered them. She had come around behind them, and although the boat was going heck-for-leather, battering its way through the light chop, sending spray everywhere, and despite the fact that Mack had a sneaking suspicion that Stefan was having the time of his life, Mack said to Xiao, "Together. Let's try it."

He took her hand. He didn't actually feel it, but he took it. And together they cried, "*A-ma belast dafee!*"

It didn't happen all at once.

Nessie was rearing up ready to smash the stern and probably kill the engines, leaving them helpless, when feathers suddenly rippled all across her rubbery, reptilian flesh.

Nessie didn't notice right away. But it was hard to miss if you were watching in wide-eyed terror.

Then her toothy dinosaur jaw began to stretch and flatten.

That, Nessie noticed.

And she noticed the way her forward fin-arms melted and were then covered with feathers.

"That's not rocks!" Xiao cried.

And Nessie's rear fins spread wide and became leathery triangles. In fact, became the world's largest duck feet.

In desperation she lashed her tail forward, snapping it like a bullwhip. But in midsnap the tail shrank and disappeared altogether.

The boat roared away as Nessie fell behind.

She was a duck. A very, very big duck.

"Oh," Mack said. "Now I see it: the long rock is the body and the little rock is a head and . . . ah."

Nessie, her eyes filling with horror and frustration, let loose a terrifying cry of hatred. "QUACK!"

Stefan slowed the engines when they were a few hundred yards away. Mack and Xiao crept into the shattered cabin to find a bloody but unbowed Dietmar and a battered but defiant Sylvie.

The shaken, drenched Magnifica stared in amazement at a duck the size of a cabin cruiser.

The fight was gone from the All-Mother.

Jarrah looked sidelong at Xiao and Mack. "Did you guys mean to turn her into a duck?"

Together Xiao and Mack nodded. "Yes. Absolutely."

"Because?" Jarrah asked.

"Plenty of time to discuss that later," Mack said. "Stefan," he yelled up to his friend. "Take us back to the dock. We need a hospital."

In despair, realizing now that she would likely never be free to wreak revenge, the duck-formerly-known-as-Nessie let go a pitiful quack of sadness.

And what is sadder than a sad, sad quack?

Fourteen

MEANWHILE, IN SEDONA, ARIZONA

The golem was sent home for largeness.

There had never been a kid sent home for largeness in the history of Richard Gere Middle School.[21] Then again, no other kid had ever broken the Chair of Doom.

The office staff had called the school custodian to unbolt the desk and remove it from around

---

21 Ha! Tricked you. Made you look at the footnote even though it doesn't say, "Go, Fighting Pupfish." Oh, wait, now it kind of does.

the golem's waist. It now lay in pieces. That was not the Chair of Doom, that was just the Desk of Disassembly.

The Chair of Doom was what kids called the chair placed directly in front of the assistant principal's desk. It was the chair you sat in when you were in trouble and about to be expelled, suspended, assigned extra study hall, or, in a harsh punishment unique to RGMS, forced to endure an hour of hot yoga.

The golem had managed to wedge his largeness into the chair. But he had continued getting bigger as he sat there, and soon the arms of the chair pushed outward. And then the legs collapsed.

Then the golem jumped up out of the collapsed chair and smacked his huge head into the ceiling tiles.

Here's the thing you need to know about assistant principals: they are usually responsible for discipline. But very few of them are prepared to deal with supernatural phenomena. Coping with violations of the Laws of Nature was not the purpose of the Chair of Doom.

So the golem was sent home.

He lumbered happily along the street, enjoying the totally new perspective he was getting: he could see the upper branches of trees now. And enjoying, too, the *crunch crunch crunch* of the cracking cement in the sidewalk.

Mack's mother had been called and she was on her way to meet him. And frankly, the golem wasn't looking forward to it. He liked Mom—well, Mack's mom—in fact he wished sometimes she really was his mom. After all, he'd never had a mom. Or a dad. In any case, though, he wasn't looking forward to it because he had the sense that possibly he worried Mom a little. And he had the feeling that being sent home from school would worry her more.

When he reached the house, Mom was just pulling into the driveway in her hybrid crossover vehicle.[22]

The golem gave a cheerful wave.

The hybrid crossover vehicle came to a stop in the driveway. Mom stepped out.

And then a girl the golem had never seen before stepped out of the passenger side.

The girl and Mom were chatting somewhat awkwardly. The golem was no judge of ages but he guessed the girl was maybe sixteen or eighteen years old. She had amazing red hair, and even more amazing green

---

22 Definitely not a minivan. This was Sedona, after all.

eyes. He was pretty sure she was beautiful, though again: he was not a great expert on female beauty. She was dressed in a very mature, grown-up, Nordstrom sort of way, very businessy.

Mom was saying, "I really do hope you'll stay for dinner, Risky."

And the girl or young woman, Risky, was eyeing the golem with amusement. "So this is your son? Mack, was it? Are you Mack?" She addressed that last part to the golem.

"I'm Mack," the golem said, feeling just the slightest reluctance to talk to her. He didn't have a lot of experience with people and therefore he was usually inclined to think that people were basically good.

But this girl didn't seem good.

Also, despite the fact that her clothing fit her perfectly, she didn't seem to fit the clothing. It was like when you see a monkey wearing pants. Only in this case it was like seeing a crocodile wearing a business suit: the outfit may say, "Safe," but the eyes said, "Danger."

"I'm a big boy," the golem said.

"I have got to stop feeding him," Mom said.

Risky gave a knowing little laugh. "Oh, I doubt that would have much effect. But I bet I can slim him right down."

"Diet and exercise?" Mom suggested.

"That never works," Risky said. "Except in rare cases where people actually eat less and exercise. No, I have a better way. A more . . . high-tech way. It turns out there's an app for that." She pulled a smartphone from her purse. Two, actually.

"I don't see how an app . . . ," Mom said doubtfully.

"Silence, fool!" Risky snarled. Then, "I mean . . . trust me."

"Mack," Mom said, "I happened to meet this young lady at the salon. I started telling her about you. About some of the . . . well, the issues . . . we've had lately. She's already at the university and doing a paper on . . . On what is it, Risky?"

Risky smiled, showing too many brilliant white teeth. "I'm doing a paper on pseudosupernatural phenomena. Things that seem to be supernatural, hard to explain, but are really quite normal."

"She thinks you're probably quite normal, sweetie." Mom said this with such a mix of hope and love and lingering fear that, well, if the golem had had a heart, it would have swelled.

As it was, the rest of him was still swelling.

Risky was finished thumbing the phone. She smiled up at the golem and said, "Just put this in your mouth." And she held the phone out to him.

Nothing about this seemed the slightest bit strange to the golem, of course, but Mom was a different story. She had her doubts and she said so in no uncertain terms. "I hope this app is suitable for his age group."

"Everything I do is suitable," Risky said.

The golem put the phone in his mouth and began to chew.

"No! Don't bite it!" Risky said. "Just hold it in your mouth." Then she thumbed a text message into her own phone and hit Send. Seconds later, the phone in the golem's mouth chimed as the text arrived.

And suddenly the golem began to shrink. His giant Popeye forearms deflated to become Mack's relatively puny arms. His ankles no longer popped out of his shoes like mutant muffins. His belly was once more flat and he could no longer see the tops of everyone's heads.

"That is a very impressive app," Mom said. The golem noticed something about Mom then: her eyes weren't quite looking at him, they were looking past him. And her voice had a dreamy sound to it. Maybe she was tired.

The golem took the phone out of his mouth and held it out to Risky. He noticed that the only thing on the screen was a standard text box. It read, "Shrink back to your normal size."

Just that. Just words.

"No, keep that phone, please," Risky said. "Be sure to answer it if it ever rings." Then she leaned in close and said, "And don't forget to do whatever the voice tells you to do." She winked at him and then, rather belatedly, said, "I'd love to stay to dinner. In fact, I can't wait to get to know your whole family."

Later, the golem sent Mack a text.

> I'm not a big boy anymore but I am perfectly normal.

He had used the phone to take a picture of Risky sitting at the family dinner table. Risky had been charming throughout dinner (chicken piccata with spaghettini) and very pleasant to the golem.

"How do I send you a picture?" he texted. Because as charming as the red-haired girl was, there was something about her. . . .

In fact, he'd had to take two pictures to get one good one. The first one had some kind of problem: it showed Mom and Dad and, seated between them, something very like a monster. A monster wearing a linen business suit and just-this-side-of-Gaga high heels.

The second shot, the one Risky had noticed him taking, showed her as she was. (Or so the golem thought.) But it all added to the golem's sense that something here was off. Weird. (And he had a very high threshold for weird.)

He wanted to send Mack that second picture. Maybe the first one, too.

"Picture?" Mack texted back. "No pictures, I'm homesick enough. Have to get on a plane to Paris. I'll be off-line anyway."

Risky had watched the golem thumb in a text and then heard the chime for incoming text.

"Is that your girlfriend?" she asked, and Mom and

Dad laughed a bit too loudly.

"No, it's just . . . just . . ." Why was it so hard to tell her a simple lie? Mack had told him many times never to reveal the truth of who he was and what was going on. He had explained the concept of lying to the golem. And the golem mostly understood, in his own way.

But there was something about her eyes. . . . When she stared at him, he almost couldn't look away.

"Tell me," Risky said, in a voice that was like a loud whisper for his ears only. As if her lips were pressed against his ear. And yet, the golem noticed, her lips never actually moved.

"It's a friend," the golem said. "On his way to Paris."

"Paris?" Risky said, and nodded as if to herself. "Of course."

Five minutes later Mom looked over at the place where Risky had been. She frowned at the plate of food, untouched. "Why on earth is there a plate of food there?"

Dad frowned as well. "I have no idea."

And that was when the golem really started to worry.

Fifteen

Fortunately, in addition to being excellent inventors, the Scots know a bit about medicine, too. The captain was patched up. Dietmar and Sylvie were treated for their not-too-serious injuries.

Cost: 0.00 GBP.[23]

It was still two days before the Magnifica managed to leave Scotland.

They drove away toward the nearest airport—in Inverness—destroying quite a number of mailboxes,

---

23 National Health Service.

lampposts, fences, and, of course, side mirrors en route.

The road they drove on was already lined with signs and billboards hastily altered to take advantage of the new situation. Everywhere they looked, "Search for the Loch Ness Monster!" had already been changed to "See the Loch Ness Duck!"

The traffic heading toward the loch was practically gridlocked.

The tourism business—which had sputtered along on one ruined castle and an elusive mythical beast—now exploded with the addition of a castle only some people could see, and a massive duck everyone could actually feed.

They never heard from Frank again. And the only thing the All-Mother had to say was a loud, furious quack.

It was a short flight to Paris. Just long enough for Mack to get Sylvie's story. (Cost of six one-way tickets to Paris: 3,023.28 GBP.[24])

She told it in excellent English and with a French accent Mack found charming. For a while he hoped that his paying attention to Sylvie would inspire some

---

24 They got hosed on last-minute tickets. And that's not even first class. Ouch.

jealousy in Xiao. But it didn't. And why he should want her to be jealous he couldn't possibly have explained. Any number of things had changed for Mack lately—he had a golem, his former bully was now his bodyguard, he was bearing enormous responsibilities, and he could apparently turn dinosaur sea serpents into giant ducks—but at the same time some much more mundane changes were taking place.

He was beginning to see the world differently. He was seeing people differently.

He was even seeing himself differently, and it was all a bit disturbing. Given that he had plenty of craziness going on, the personal changes were mostly unwelcome.

But there was no escaping the fact that he had gone from not caring about girls as anything other than a sort of subspecies of kids at school to paying slightly more attention to them and wishing they would pay slightly more attention to him.

In this he was behind the girls, who had long since begun to notice boys and had already formed some pretty definite opinions about them in general and Mack in particular.

There were many things that Vargran might cure, but boys being just a few steps behind girls was too basic a fact of life for mere magic to alter.

"I have always known that I was strange," Sylvie said as the jet rose steeply away from Inverness and arced out over the sea. "As a little girl I did not play with dolls. I did not play at all, except in my imagination. In my imagination I saw myself as a warrior, and a companion to other warriors. Strange, no? Because most little girls see themselves as princesses."

"Strange maybe," Mack allowed. "But Xiao is a dragon, so the bar is pretty high on 'strange' in this group. Dietmar was a little like you: he kind of knew something was coming, if you know what I mean."

He wanted to bite his tongue. Why would he draw her attention to Dietmar?

"How did you just happen to be in Scotland?"

"I did not 'just happen,'" Sylvie said. "It is more complicated than that. It began for me in the summer. Fouras is a village with beaches. Tourists come to swim and lie in the sun, yes?"

"*Oui*," he said, feeling self-conscious. *Oui* was pretty much the limit of his French.

"My parents have a small merry-go-round near the beach. There are restaurants and *crêperies* and souvenirs, and there is the merry-go-round. Only it is not so merry, I think. I find it melancholy. Children climb on looking for joy and find only a meaningless circular pursuit that cannot relieve the existential pain of existence, the fundamental ennui that must afflict any thinking person."

Mack had no idea what she had just said, beyond "merry-go-round," but he loved the way she said it.

"There was a boy there, one day. He was strangely dressed, flamboyant, you might say. I was collecting tickets, and he said to me, 'What is that brass ring that you taunt the children with?'

"You see," Sylvie explained, "a brass ring dangles from a rope. It is yanked here and there by my mother, or by me when I am helping. A child who rides the wooden ponies must grab the ring to get a free ride."

"Okay," Mack said, mentally filing away the fact that this must be where the phrase *grab the brass ring* came from.

"This boy said to me, 'Why should the children

strain for the bauble merely to repeat a meaningless experience that only serves to make them aware of the void that lies before them depriving life itself of any meaning?"

"So this boy was French, too?" Mack asked.

"No, he was from India. He had an accent, dark skin, and, as I said, dressed in unusual style."

Mack got a tingling on the back of his neck. "Wait a sec. It wasn't Valin, was it?"

"Yes, Mack, it was," Sylvie said, not surprised that he had guessed.

"But didn't you say he was your brother?" Mack said, and then, without waiting for Sylvie's response, added, "And doesn't he work for Paddy 'Nine Iron' Trout?"

Sylvie shrugged expressively. "He learns from the man in green, but does he serve him? Valin serves himself alone, I think."

"As long as he is working against us, he's working for the Pale Queen," Mack said sharply.

"You see the world in simple black and white? It must be us and them? Good and evil?"

"In this case, yeah," Mack said. "The Pale Queen is evil."

"How do you know this? Because the ancient Grimluk has told you?"

Mack moved back a few inches. "Okay, yes. But I've also met Risky. That girl is evil."

"You feel it here?" Sylvie lay her hand over his heart.

He nodded because he couldn't speak.

Sylvie returned that wordless gesture. "Yes. And so I felt when Valin introduced me to *l'homme en vert*, the man in green. Paddy 'Nine Iron' Trout."

"Yeah, he gives off a kind of evil vibe."

"A vibe. Yes," Sylvie said, not quite agreeing. "It was Valin who told me that I was one of the Magnificent Twelve. He told me that the strangeness of my life was because of this curse."

"Curse?" The word surprised Mack.

"Of course it is a curse. How could it be a blessing, Mack? To have power is to have responsibility. I would have to devote my life to maintaining the empty shell of existence."

"Um . . . well, I kind of guess I don't think existence is meaningless," Mack said.

That caused one of Sylvie's eyebrows to rise in amused skepticism, but she didn't respond directly.

"Valin told me all. He revealed what I had never known: that we shared a father. But Valin was obsessed with his mother's side of his family, indifferent to the father we shared. He told me that a terrible wrong had been done to his family by your people."

"Did he tell you what his beef was? Because as far as I know, my family is pretty boring."

"It was a long time ago," Sylvie said.

"Even a long time ago my family was boring."

"He did not explain this . . . as you said, beef. Instead he told me of himself and of the man in green. He told me too much, perhaps. Because as he explained, it seemed to me that I must not join him. But rather that I should fight against him."

"Wouldn't that be meaningless, too?"

"I must defend *la liberté*, liberty, no? I am French, after all."

That seemed obvious to her, and Mack was frankly so confused by Sylvie he felt it best just to keep quiet.

"Valin, he foolishly trusted me with the names of two others who he would attempt to recruit to his side."

"You beat him to those two?"

For the first time, Sylvie smiled. "Valin is very old-fashioned. He does not know email, texting, Facebook, Twitter, or Google Plus. Before he could even begin to reach the two, I had found them online. They figured out ways to come to Paris. And I went in search of you, to unite us all together."

"How did you find me?"

"You leave a trail of YouTubes behind you, Mack."

Mack thought back on the first shaky YouTube video that showed him and Stefan running from Skirrit at Richard Gere Middle School;[25] the YouTube video of him being dragged out the door of a jet by a monstrous version of Risky; the one about the swollen, bloated blue-cheese-filled Lepercons; the one some shaky tourist had filmed of the Great Wall of China. . . . Yes, he hadn't exactly concealed his tracks. It didn't seem as if the authorities had caught on yet. There were millions of hits on Mack's various inadvertent (and terrifying) videos, but the consensus of opinion was that it was all a massive game being perpetrated as part of an advertising campaign for a movie.

"Still, how could you find exactly where I was?" Mack asked. A bit of suspicion wormed at his brain.

---

25 Go, Fighting Pupfish!

Sylvie had been friends with Valin. She had met Nine Iron.

"I knew a Vargran phrase that led me to you."

"Valin taught you Vargran?"

"No, not that. Valin is not a fool. As I told you, I have always known there was something odd about me. You see, from early on I had found a Vargran artifact."

"Where? At the merry-go-round?"

She gave him a reproachful look. "Do not toy with me, Mack. No, I found it in the moat of the fort. There is a Vauban fort in Fouras. It is not so ancient, only a few centuries old. It was used under Napoléon's rule. It has a moat, but the moat has long been dry, and children climb down there to play, or to hide from the petty tyranny of bourgeois parents."

"Okay."

"One day I was down there, alone, and I felt a strange presence. I looked up, and there appeared a spectral shape. A very ancient man with green-tinged fingernails and few teeth."

"Grimluk?"

"Grimluk. He was weak and failing—"

"He always is."

"And his time was short—"

"I've heard that before."

"And when he spoke, it was in a riddle, gasping, incoherent and very hard to understand."

"That's Grimluk, all right," Mack confirmed.

"He drew my attention to a piece of stone sticking up out of the muck of the moat. Then he faded from view. I went back the next day with a toy shovel— laughable, no? I had no true shovel, only a mockery of a shovel. But I dug, Mack. I dug like a mad thing, flinging clods of mud in every direction, in a frenzy, until, with dirt-crusted fingernails, I could claw away the last of the mud and see that to the stone was attached a golden shield."

"Gold?"

"Gold does not tarnish, Mack. Not even after three thousand years. A scene was etched into that gold. It showed a terrible monster, unimaginable, huge, and surrounded by minions of a dozen horrible types. And facing them, twelve. . . . Just twelve."

"The original Magnificent Twelve," Mack said in an awestruck whisper.

"Yes. And along the edges of that depiction were

strange words written in a strange alphabet. Each day I came back to that stone. I concealed it with branches so that only I could feast greedy eyes upon it. I tried to puzzle out the words, you see. For such a long time it did not work. Then, one day, I spoke the words *flee-ma omias*. All at once the moat began to fill with water. I was terrified, of course, and more so still when I saw that the rising water was filled with panicked fish, all thrashing as though to escape the water itself. You see, I had spoken the Vargran word for 'run' and the word for 'fish.'"

"Run fish?"

"In the imperative, 'or else' tense. It was a macabre horror," Sylvie said.

"Fish trying to run away?"

"Have you ever seen a thousand panicked fish?"

"Not really."

"It is something you will never forget. I climbed the vines to escape the moat. I thought it was a hallucination. But the next day the town was abuzz with the miracle of fish appearing suddenly in the moat. Dead of course, since the water soon seeped away. The smell was very bad."

"It would be."

"It was weeks before I ventured into the moat again. But with those first words I was able to unravel the meaning of the remaining words. I learned perhaps two dozen Vargran words."

"You learned enough to save my life," Mack said.

"Also enough to know that Valin was tricking me. For, you see, he refused to teach me any Vargran himself. He only wished to neutralize me, to use me to find others, and thus destroy you and your mission."

"He must really not be very happy with you, and I guess you don't like him much," Mack said, probing for any lingering loyalty she might have for her half brother.

But her eyes blazed with sudden fury. "Why do you think I traveled to Scotland with my grandparents and not my mother and father?"

"I—"

"Valin!" She spit the word out like it was a bad olive pit. "He sought to control me by placing a Vargran spell on my parents."

"What spell?"

"My parents are no longer merely the owners of

the merry-go-round," she said. "My father is one of the wooden horses. My mother is a wooden swan."

Mack felt as if his heart had stopped. And he had been suspicious of her.

"They go round and round now, in a meaningless dance to music they cannot hear, twirling through the void."

At which point, with a shuddering thud, the jet touched down at Charles de Gaulle Airport, outside Paris.

Sixteen

Mack, Jarrah, Dietmar, Xiao, Sylvie, and Stefan took the train from the airport into the city. Needless to say, none of them had ever been to Paris before, except for Sylvie.

It's quite a city.

You start with the river that runs through it: the Seine. It's a moderately large river, much more than a stream, but not quite the Mississippi, either. It doesn't hurry, but it doesn't meander. It sort of chugs along.

There are lots of bridges, most fairly modest but

some with golden lion statues and whatnot. There are lots of boats—barges and tugboats and especially the *bateaux mouches*, which are amazingly long and narrow and usually glass-bubbled with tourists staring out at the city.

In the middle of the river is a pair of islands, one of which is home to the Gothic cathedral of Notre-Dame—a very Hunchback of Notre-Dame kind of place.

There's the Arc de Triomphe, which is a sort of massive stone arch marooned in the middle of a crazy traffic circle with about nine different roads coming in.

But the most identifiable sight in Paris is the Eiffel Tower. When the Eiffel Tower was first built (coincidentally by a guy named Eiffel, what are the odds?) everyone was all like, "Man, that sucks." Or in French, "*Mais, que cela sucks, n'est-ce pas?*"

The problem was that the Eiffel Tower looked like it was made out of an Erector set, which was what kids played with before the invention of Legos, which was what kids played with before the invention of iPad games.

But over time people were like, "Maybe we were hasty in saying it sucks."

Followed by, "It's actually not bad."

Followed by, "It's epic!"

Followed by, "Are you dissing my tower? Because I will totally kick your butt!"

The tower is visible from just about anywhere in Paris. It will be at the end of an avenue, or you'll be floating down the river and, hey, there it is, or maybe you'll see the top poking above a building. It's ubiquitous. It's a cliché.

You know what else it is? Beautiful. Especially at night when it's lit up.

So anyway, add in a bunch of sidewalk cafés, the Métro, a few more churches, a scattering of museums, and you basically have Paris. So now you don't even have to go, you've already experienced it.

One other interesting feature of Paris: the sewers.

Back in days of yore (say a thousand years ago, round numbers), when Paris was growing larger, people were saying, "Hey, we don't have sewers, so we're dumping our poop into the streets. Also our unused chunks of butchered hog, our dead rats, our rotted fruit, our three hundred and fifty-two kinds of cheese rind, and of course, during plague years,[26] our dead relatives. The result is, shall we say, not as pleasantly fragrant as a nice glass of *vin rouge*."

Yes: they noticed that poop and dead things smelled.

So they built sewers, giant underground tunnels. That way, the fecal matter and dead things that got dumped in the street eventually sloshed down into the sewers, which helpfully carried such things to the river. The same river whose water people drank. So they quickly went from, "Man, the air stinks," to, "Man, this water tastes awful. Plus, I'm sick now."

Hey, it was medieval times. It took a while for people to figure stuff out in those days.

Anyway, the sewers are no longer in use much except for when it rains and the water goes rushing through the ancient tunnels. In fact, now you can take a tour of the sewers. People do.

Cost of Paris sewer tour for six kids: 24 euros.[27]

"We are being followed," Dietmar said as the Magnificent Five (so far) emerged from the train station weary and worried.

---

26 Pretty much every year in medieval and Renaissance times.

27 Also a type of money, but less so.

"The guy in the trench coat?" Mack asked. Because Mack had also noticed the person in the trench coat with the hat pulled down low over his brow.

It was night and the city was lit up but not so well lit as to banish all shadows. The trench coat seemed to be staying with those shadows, circling wide around bright-lit cafés and melting into closed-down shop fronts.

"Yes," Dietmar confirmed. "There is something strange about him."

"Yeah," Mack confirmed, feeling a tightening in his throat. "Very strange for a man, not strange at all for a Skirrit. And there's another one across the street."

"They've spotted us already?" Sylvie asked. "That is bad. I had hoped to take you straight to the sewers."

"Sewers? I was hoping for a hotel. And a sandwich," Jarrah said.

"We have a hotel," Mack said. "The trick will be getting there alive."

"Surely they wouldn't attack us right out in the open on a Paris street?" Xiao said.

Sylvie said, "They are not attacking, they are following. They want us to lead them to the others."

Mack decided that was probably right. It was also probably true that Skirrit—even ones with hats—would be noticed in a brightly lit, crowded place.

"I doubt they can follow us down into the Métro," Mack said. They were walking on the rue La Fayette, which was not one of the biggest, widest avenues, but a respectably important street. But it was late, and only a few restaurants and cafés were open.

"I have a Métro app," Sylvie offered. "I don't live in Paris so I don't know the system. But there is a stop—Poissonnière. I know we need to get to Alma-Marceau. . . ."

She began thumbing information into the app.

"Okay, then, we take the Seven line and switch to the Nine line," Sylvie said decisively.

"We'll follow you."

Down the narrow, dirty stairs into the station: white tile, cement floor, modern ticket-vending machines. They used the million-dollar credit card to buy six tickets.[28] This took a while. And during that while, the Skirrit came down the stairs after them.

---

28 10.2 euros. They could have gotten a *carnet* of ten tickets for just 12.50, but what good would that do?

As Dietmar handed out tickets, two Skirrit stared and twitched nervously in their weak disguises.

In the unlikely event that you don't know what a Skirrit is, think grasshopper or maybe praying mantis, but about the height of a moderately short man, and walking erect.

Parisians, being city people, seldom look anyone in the face, so it seemed possible to Mack that the Skirrit might go unnoticed. They might even wait until the crowd had thinned a little and—

"Aaaahhh!" An older woman, built like a fireplug but with an attractive scarf around her throat, pointed in horror at a face that did not belong on anything human.

The Skirrit drew a knife from under its trench coat and seemed ready to go for the woman to silence her.

"Hey!" Mack yelled. "This is between us."

The Skirrit's expressionless insect eyes turned to glare at him. The knife wavered. The woman ran. The Skirrit hissed, then turned and quickly ran with his companion up the stairs.

"That was easy," Jarrah said, sounding slightly disappointed.

"That was both brave and self-sacrificing, Mack," Xiao said, sounding a bit too surprised.

"Let's get out of here," Mack said. He was troubled. Jarrah was right, it had been easy. Too easy.

They passed their tickets through the ticket reader and found their way to the right platform. The light was cold and gray. The white tile was grimy. The only color came from large posters that followed the curve of the walls and advertised banks, tours, sneakers, and movies.

The train came in a whoosh of fetid air and screeched to a stop. Doors opened. Glum-faced people stepped off. Other glum-faced people got on, along with Mack and his friends.

The train was crowded—standing room only—which seemed odd this late. Maybe all the people were coming from some special event.

The six kids were soon separated. Mack found himself clinging to a chrome pole he had to share with four other hands. People pressed close around him as the train lurched away from the station.

Mack felt a hand touch his on the rail.

He moved his hand away an inch (or 2.5 centimeters since it's France).

This time the hand—a delicate, pale, female hand—covered his. He followed the hand to the wrist. Then the wrist to the arm. The arm to the shoulder. To those eyes. Those impossibly green eyes.

"*Bonjour*, Mack," Risky said.

Seventeen

MEANWHILE, IN MACK'S BEDROOM IN SEDONA

The golem lay on the wall of Mack's room. He had never gotten entirely used to sleeping on the bed. Or horizontally. There was just something about lying flat against a wall that felt comfortable and right.

But this night he was having a hard time getting to sleep. He was tossing and turning, sometimes rolling all the way up to the ceiling.

The golem wasn't a thoughtful creature.[29] He didn't normally lie awake wondering what to do about the deficit or pondering the nature of existence or wondering why any human being would willingly consume CornNuts.

He was not a philosopher, and those questions were beyond him.

But the encounter with Risky had gotten him thinking. There was something wrong about that girl. The thing she had done with the phone in his mouth . . . He hadn't decided to shrink back to normal; she had sent a text and it had worked just like the scroll that Grimluk had placed in his mouth at the moment of his completion.

He still had the phone. It was sitting on his—Mack's—desk. He wondered if she would ever call him.

He wondered if he would be able to resist if she told him to put the phone in his mouth.

He wondered whether he would have to become whatever she texted.

The idea was troubling. The golem furrowed his

---

29 This is known as "understatement."

brow, a phrase he had learned in school. He furrowed his brow thoughtfully, and then became distracted for a while with the realization that furrows are what farmers form in the fields. They plant corn and soybeans and beets[30] in the furrows. And should he try doing that with the furrows in his forehead? Would Camaro be impressed that he could grow tiny corn in his forehead?

Thinking of Camaro just made him toss and turn some more, and he finally got up and paced around the ceiling for a while. He had promised to be a "big boy" when she did something—he wasn't quite clear on what—with Tony Pooch.

Now he was no longer a big boy. Although maybe he could become big again. He thought about testing it out, growing a little. But he was afraid to try. What if it didn't work?

In some strange way, Risky taking him over had changed his outlook on life. He'd always been content to just "Be Mack." Those were the words on the scroll, and he had never questioned them.

But now . . . now he had been forced to change, and

---

30 No one knows why the beets.

that changing thing, becoming something different—even for just a while as he shrank—had broadened his outlook. It had introduced . . . possibilities.

If she called . . . he would try not to obey.

What a crazy thought! How could a mere golem refuse to obey the words of power placed in his mouth?

But he would have to try, wouldn't he?

He lay back down again, snuggled between two wall posters.

Be Mack.

He was doing that as well as he could. He would do that until Mack returned. And then . . .

Oh, right: then he would return to the mud he had been fashioned from.

Unless of course she called.

Eighteen

"So close, eh, Mack?" she asked.

"Close?" he squeaked.

"Already you have assembled five. And more await here in Paris. *N'est-ce pas?* As the locals would say?"

"Are you going to kill me?"

That got the attention of some of the passengers nearby. One man cast a very suspicious look at Mack.

"Kill you?" Risky echoed. "Wherever did you get that idea?"

"I think maybe it was because you tried to kill

me before. Several times."

"Oh, yes," she said, and gazed off into space as if she was savoring the memories. "Good times. Good times. By the way, don't you want to know how I found you?"

"By . . . supernatural means. You always seem to find me."

"Paddy had lost track of you after Stonehenge. You were completely off the grid. Then we heard you were in Scotland."

"How did you hear that?"

Risky shrugged. "Twitter. It was a trending topic. But I found out too late; I don't check Twitter as often as I should."

"How many Twitter followers do you have?" Mack asked, aware that the conversation had taken a rather odd turn.

"Four," Risky admitted.

"You should tweet more. That's the only way."

"I should be tweeting right now," Risky agreed. "I could say, 'Found Mack in Paris thanks to—'"

And that's when the train reached the next station and the brakes screeched so loud that Mack heard none of what Risky had to say.

The doors opened. It wasn't Mack's stop, but he really wanted to get off anyway. Get off and then run screaming down the platform, up the escalator, and onto the street.

But he didn't do any of that. In the movement of bodies on and off the train, Dietmar was suddenly closer. He hadn't noticed that Mack was talking to Risky.

"We must get off in two stops and then switch to the—"

Dietmar stopped talking when Mack made a quick throat-cutting gesture. Then he noticed Risky. She gave him a dazzling smile.

Dietmar did not smile back.

"Is this . . . ?" Dietmar asked before his voice dried up.

"My friends call me Risky," she said. "But I have many names."

"And no friends," Mack said.

"You know, I do have feelings, Mack, and that hurts."

Mack almost apologized but managed to stop himself. She had no feelings. At least no decent, normal feelings. She was an evil creature. It was just that the red hair and the green eyes and the whole bewitching-beauty thing made her seem like she might have feelings. For just a second. But no: she didn't.

And the little glistening tear that appeared in her eye was fake.

"I have to tell you, Mack, I've changed," Risky said.

"Changed?"

"I have come to realize that my mother . . ." She paused, glanced at Dietmar, and explained, "My mother, the Pale Queen."

Dietmar nodded. "Yes, I understood that."

"Clever boy. Anyway, I have come to realize that my mother should not be allowed to emerge and crush all life under her heel and enslave all of humanity to her evil will."

"No?" Mack asked.

"No. Instead, I should crush all life under my heel and enslave all of humanity to my evil will."

"How would that be better?" Mack asked.

"Because it would be me," Risky said, and added, "I thought that was self-explanatory."

Dietmar said, "We don't want to be crushed or

enslaved by anyone."

And Mack was left to say, "He's right."

"Then you'll like this part," Risky said in a con-spiratorial voice. "I am willing to let you, Mack, and your little friends be my personal household ser-vants."

"No thanks," Mack said quickly, trying to speak before Dietmar had a chance.

Risky ignored him. "It's a good job. All you would really have to do is help me deal with Mom."

"How would we even do that?" Mack asked.

Risky smiled, but it wasn't her dazzling smile, it was a crafty and cruel smile. "You have the Key. I know you have the Key, Mack. Once you master it, you will have great power."

"Great enough to defeat the Pale Queen—and you!" Dietmar said a bit fervently.

Another stop. More people on and off. And now Xiao moved close enough to see who Mack and Dietmar were talking to.

"Oh, it's the littlest dragon," Risky snarked.

"Ereskigal," Xiao said darkly.

"Guilty," Risky admitted. "So very guilty. Now

be a good little reptile and let me talk to Mack and Dirtmore here."

"Dietmar," Dietmar corrected.

"Yes, the Key gives you great power. But not enough to stop my mother—not unless you truly become the Twelve. Right now you're the Five. Maybe you can save the two here in Paris—although I doubt it—and then you would be the Seven. That leaves five, Mack. And one of those is already my servant."

The thing was, Mack was starting to worry, because she was making sense. The odds were ridiculous. And even Grimluk had made clear that it would take the united power of all twelve to defeat the Pale Queen.

Was this a hopeless mission? Was he doomed to defeat anyway?

And could he possibly, somehow, maybe, work out a deal with Risky? Wouldn't it be better to have her crushing all of humanity beneath her boot rather than her mother doing it? At the very least, it would mean one evil tyrant rather than two. That had to be an improvement.

"You will never turn Valin to your side, Mack," she purred, seeing his hesitancy. "He is ours. So there will never be a Twelve. Perhaps you can fantasize about an Eleven, but never a Twelve. In the end you will be defeated. Unless . . ."

"She is trying to weaken you," Xiao said.

"I'm trying to help him, annoying little dragon person," Risky said. "Join me, Mack. Join me, and no harm will come to you and yours. Your family will be safe."

With that, the mask of sweetness seemed to fall from Risky's face. Because that was a threat she was making.

"My family?" Mack said.

"Your family, your town, your school," Risky said. "Go, Fighting Pupfish, right? Figure it out, Mack. Put two and two together."

"I . . . what?"

"Give me the Key and join me," Risky said.

Mack hesitated. Just for a moment, but long enough to earn a hard look from Dietmar and Xiao.

"I'll never join you, Risky," Mack said finally. "And this is our stop."

Risky shrugged. "We'll see."

And with that, she disappeared.

The train pulled into the station.

They switched trains, and Risky was not on this one. There wasn't much of a crowd, and the six of them were able to sit close together.

"We have twenty-eight days left," Mack said, shouting a bit to be heard over the frantic squeal of brakes and the rattle of the train as it turned a corner in its dark tunnel. "If we can save Sylvie's friends—"

"They are not friends. They are Magnifica, but I don't know them well."

"Great," Stefan muttered.

"What are their names so we can stop calling them just 'your friends'?" Jarrah said.

"One is called Rodrigo. He is from Argentina. The other is Charlie. He's English."

Mack frowned. "I'm trying to find some pattern. It's like the Magnifica are spread all over the world. The United States, France, China, Australia, Germany, now Argentina and England. Plus India, where Valin is from." He looked to Sylvie so she could explain.

"Valin is my half brother, but he is from India," Sylvie said. "Our father was a French diplomat. Valin's mother is Indian, and he was raised in the Punjab. Her family is from somewhere in the interior. It was there that in ancient times Mack's family did a terrible wrong to Valin's mother's family."

Mack made a frustrated *grrrr* sound. "My family isn't even ancient; how could they have done something evil to people in India? Like I said, we're boring! We live in Arizona!" Mack protested.

"We have Indians in Arizona," Stefan pointed out. He had come up behind Mack.

"Different Indians," Mack snapped, and then his phone chimed and he made the frustrated *grrr* sound again. He did not have time for more idiocy from the golem.

"This is our stop," Dietmar said.

They got off the train and started to head up the escalator to the outside world. Suddenly Mack stopped them. He drew them aside into a connecting tunnel, where a woman played a mournful tune on her violin and collected donations in the open case.

"Listen, we have the Key now. So how about for once we do the smart thing and actually take a few minutes to learn some useful spells? You know, before we run into whatever gauntlet Risky has prepared for us outside."

"Yes," Dietmar seconded enthusiastically.

"Awww, homework?" Jarrah moaned. But then she sighed and said, "All right then. A bit of Vargran can't hurt."

It was fifteen minutes before the Five plus Stefan emerged from the Métro stop. And when they stepped into the glittering Paris night near the hectic traffic free-for-all at the head of the Pont de l'Alma, the Alma Bridge, they were a different bunch of kids than they had been before.

Nineteen

They emerged from the Métro.

Now, no one is saying they looked like, oh, the Magnificent Seven from that movie, all riding their horses and seeming tough.

No one is saying they were six little Bournes, each a human killing machine. No one is drawing any parallels to the Avengers. (The kids had met Thor, and real Thor was nothing like movie Thor.)

But they were prepared for once. Ready for battle.

Oh, yeah: they were ready.

Their first battle was getting across traffic to the bridge. Their foes were many and they were armed with bright headlights and horns and French cursing.

The Magnificent Five plus Stefan made it finally onto the bridge. The entry point to the sewers where Rodrigo and Charlie were hiding was on the other side.

The bridge itself was kind of a "meh" bridge. Not much fanciness, just a lot of cars. But there were nice pedestrian walkways, too, and our intrepid heroes walked across that bridge until they reached the statues of the giants.

Wait. If the bridge—Pont de l'Alma—was so boring and "meh," what's this about giants?

Well, none of the Magnificent Five plus Stefan was that familiar with Paris—not even Sylvie, who was French but not Parisian. So for all they knew, the bridge was famous for its statues of giants.

Furry giants.

White-furred giants that had just clambered up onto the bridge from down below as they sensed the approach of the Magnifica.

But by the time Mack noticed them, they were standing stock-still, one on either side of the bridge, and his first thought was, Cool.

Then his second thought was that traffic was slowing down and people with serious trout mouth were staring in amazement. Local people don't stare at familiar landmarks. It's a fact that no Washingtonian has ever seen the Capitol building and no San Franciscan has ever noticed the Golden Gate Bridge and no New Yorker has ever looked up at a video billboard in Times Square.

So no way a bunch of Parisians were staring in jaw-dropped amazement at statues that were actually supposed to be there.

"Look out!" Mack yelled.

Everyone stopped except Dietmar, who kept loping along. He was reaching out his hand to touch the nearest of the giants, no doubt wondering how a statue could be made to appear so realistically furry.

The giant was about twenty-five feet tall, about five Macks or four Stefans or not quite six Sylvies.

It was covered with fur like a polar bear's except that it was turning a shade of pink. It had a massive head that was not bearlike but more feline, albeit with an enormous mouth filled with enormous teeth.

It had two legs like tree trunks and two arms like slightly smaller tree trunks, and hands that were three-fingered claws, each claw like one of those engraved sperm whale[31] teeth you sometimes see in nautical-themed stores.

It was a Gudridan. They both were. And although Mack had heard that word before, he didn't know to connect it to these monsters.

"Dietmar! Stop!" Mack cried.

Too late. The Gudridan's hand swung around like a boxer throwing a haymaker. The massive hand snatched Dietmar up and held him effortlessly as he strained, punched, and yelled.

Mack had a terrible vision of what would happen next. The Gudridan would slam Dietmar against the concrete, and that would be the end.

Down in the Métro they had each used the Key to learn one Vargran spell. They had twisted the smaller wheel inside the larger wheel. They had stared rather stupidly at various inexplicable symbols. And then they had heard the Vargran words in their heads, as only those with the *enlightened puissance* could. And they had memorized some of what they heard. Not

---

31 Okay, if you giggled when you read *sperm whale*, go sit in the corner.

saying they memorized it all perfectly, but they had the gist.

But they had learned that magic can't just be fired off willy-nilly like using a machine gun. Because the true power was in the *enlightened puissance* that each of them possessed. And that was like a battery that needed recharging.

So they had vowed to resist using Vargran until there was no other choice, until absolutely necessary.

This looked pretty necessary.

But it was Xiao who rushed forward and cried, "*Pu kip-ma isnyke!*" Which meant roughly, "Hey, you: put him down or else."

The Gudridan did a double take, stared down at Xiao, blinked, and dropped Dietmar. The fall was from twenty-five feet, which is about like falling off the peak of a suburban two-story home's roof.

It could easily have killed Dietmar. Except that the Gudridan was arched back and waving the boy high over its head, so when it released Dietmar, Dietmar fell into the river.

"Ahhhh . . ."

Splash!

No time to check on him, no time to worry whether

the boy could swim, because the Gudridan lashed out at Xiao with a surprisingly swift and amazingly powerful kick.

Xiao dodged, quick as a snake, and the massive foot flew past.

Now the second giant was crossing the bridge. In the flash of headlights Mack saw that its fur was no longer white but shading into pink and possibly heading toward red.

Mack didn't know this, but a Gudridan's fur changes color with its mood. The madder it is, the redder it gets. And no one has ever—ever—met a red Gudridan and lived to offer descriptions.

REDDER

www.themag12.com

Xiao was up on her feet but wobbly, and Jarrah grabbed her hand and yanked her away, heading in a mad rush toward the far side of the river. Dietmar's cries floated up from below.

The Gudridan leaped.

It was impossible to imagine. It leaped as easily as a gymnast, that gigantic thing, and landed so hard the bridge rocked. It landed clear beyond Xiao and Jarrah, blocking their path.

The second Gudridan kicked aside a Fiat 500 like it was a football. The car rolled twice and hit the stone railing and came to a stop on its side. Traffic in both directions screeched and slammed. That second Gudridan now focused on Mack. It raised its giant feet and stomped. Stomped. Stomped again, each massive hammer blow causing the bridge to shake. It was trying to crush Mack; too angry to waste time grabbing him, it wanted to stomp Mack into strawberry jam.

Mack dodged and tripped over his own feet, which sent him plowing forward. A foot slammed beside him and struck a glancing blow against his shoulder. It was like being hit by a truck. Mack went flying into the road. Had traffic not already stopped, he'd have been run over, killed instantly.

Dazed and numb on his left side, Mack rolled to his feet, stumbled, and smashed face-first into a car's hood.

He made eye contact with the driver, a middle-aged man with an astonished and offended look on his face, just as the Gudridan made a grab for Mack.

Mack jerked back, and the claw bit into the car's

sheet metal like it was Play-Doh.

Okay, time for some Vargran, Mack told himself, but his brain wasn't working too clearly now. He heard a scream. He saw Stefan, suddenly revealed in a beam of light, armed with nothing but his fists and swinging like a madman at a Gudridan's knee.

Get them all together, all but Dietmar, Mack's brain told him, and unite them in a Vargran curse. But oh, it is so much easier to think that than to do it while one of your crew is yelling and gurgling in the dark waters of the Seine, and your bodyguard has just been casually kicked aside to land like a rag doll, and a reckless Aussie has thrown her arms in a bear hug around a monster's leg, and a tiny goth girl is wiping the blood from her mouth, and a dragon in human form is crawling away across the concrete.

Things had gone very bad, very fast.

Stefan was up and racing to the Fiat, which still lay on its side. With brute force he yanked the car back onto its wheels and pulled open the twisted door while the car was still rocking.

Mack saw what he was up to. He also saw the first Gudridan take one giant step, reach down, and knock Stefan flat.

No time to think, Mack raced for the car, jumped over Stefan's horizontal form, and slid into the seat. The engine was still running! He twisted the wheel and stomped on the gas. Nothing!

Stupid gears!

Mack pushed down the clutch, rammed the car into gear, stomped on the gas, and *bam*—into the leg of the closest Gudridan.

The air bag exploded in his face, almost knocking him silly in its attempt to save him.

A roar of rage!

A bellow of pain!

Like ten lions together at feeding time when they really, really want some meat, the Gudridan's outrage shook every living thing within a mile. It was awful and awesome.

Mack's windshield was filled almost entirely by a single leg. A single leg now turning from pink to red.

To redder.

Mack jammed the car into reverse. Even in the midst of panic, a small part of his mind was thinking, Hey, I can drive as well as Stefan.

The car lurched back, sputtered, and stalled.

So maybe he wasn't a great driver, either.

He started the car again, put it in gear, and rammed the Gudridan.

Smash!

Back. And again.

Smash!

This time the Gudridan had sidestepped, but Mack twisted the wheel and caught it in the Achilles tendon. Or at the least the Gudridan equivalent.

The knee buckled.

"YAAAAAARRRGGGHHH!" the Gudridan roared.

The second Gudridan was bounding over to help its friend/companion/homey/colleague when shots rang out.

They always say that, don't they? "Shots rang out." But shots don't actually "ring;" they explode.

Blam blam blam!

A man in the natty uniform of the gendarmes was calmly firing up at the second Gudridan's head even as the first tottered like a felled tree in a national forest.

It seemed to take forever for the first monster to fall, and all the while, *blam blam blam* continued, accompanied by stabs of bright orange.

Brave gendarme.

Unfortunately, bullets don't matter much to Gudridan.

As the first of the monsters hit the ground so hard that stopped cars jumped from the impact, the second Gudridan snatched up the policeman, opened its hideous jaws, and bit off the top half of his body.

For a terrible, frozen moment, Mack just stared.

It was the most awful thing he had ever seen. And it was somehow his fault.

Mack climbed out of the car.

The Gudridan, still standing, red fur even redder from its gruesome meal, almost smiled at him.

"*Gope-ma et stib-il belast!*" Mack snarled.

Sometimes terror kind of shuts off your brain.

Other times it focuses your thoughts.

Mack had just crossed the line into focused. Very focused.

The Gudridan's red fur began to turn black in patches. The monster noticed, held up an arm to examine it, and seemed almost to whimper.

Its fur faded from red to pink, but what mattered was the creeping black growth that spread over the monster, here, there, surrounding and then absorbing fur now gone white, seeming to eat it up.

Eating then into the skin beneath the fur.

The Gudridan hollered in incoherent terror, and Mack thought, Yeah. Yeah, that's what I can bring. I can bring rot and make you die, monster! I can do that.

It was like watching time-lapse videography of an orange being consumed by mold.

The creature's fur was gone, replaced by the creeping mold. Its arms withered. Its legs were pins. It fell facedown across several cars.

The other monster, the one Mack had smashed with the car, began backpedaling frantically.

It had never seen such a thing. It had never seen one of its kind brought down by a skinny, curly-haired child spouting an ancient, forgotten language.

More gendarmes and regular cops were arriving in a festival of flashing blue lights and frantic sirens. More gunfire. The Paris night was a battlefield.

Mack ran to the rail and saw that Dietmar had swum to the far bank and was painfully hauling himself up onto the slick, wet stones.

"Everyone!" Mack yelled in a voice that was approximately one-millionth as strong as a bellowing Gudridan. "Come on!"

They formed up around him, Stefan limping and holding his side, Jarrah picking Gudridan fur out of her teeth, Sylvie and Xiao looking bruised and disheveled.

"Dietmar is across. We run for it and hope the cops think we're just normal people running for our lives!"

Which is what they did.

And what the French police assumed as they fired steadily into the back of the retreating monster.

The battered kids joined a wet and slimy Dietmar and raced shivering and heartsick toward the entryway to the Paris sewers.

Twenty

MEANWHILE, BACK IN SEDONA

The golem climbed down from the wall.

He walked to his—Mack's—desk and picked up his iPhone. Mack had told him not to bother him, that he should be a big boy and take care of himself.

But the golem was having a very bad feeling down in the muddy hole he'd dug out of himself that now functioned as a stomach.

He wrote a text to Mack.

> I'm afraid. A girl named Risky was here. I think she will make me hurt people. Your golem.

He considered adding a smiley face. He often did that. But it felt wrong. So he typed: >:-(

And he hit Send.

The text went flying through the air, from Sedona to Paris. Where the cell phone signal failed to penetrate the deep, stony sewers.

Twenty-one

The sewer tunnels are bigger than you think. Some of them are so big they could practically be Métro tunnels. Others are narrower, or crammed full of dripping metal pipes that run along the arched stone ceilings.

The parts of the sewers that are on the tour are safe and well lit. There are metal catwalks and railings. There are signs pointing toward the exits.

But that's just the part that's on the tour. There are miles and miles of sewer tunnels. (And beyond the sewer tunnels, connected to them here and there, are the tunnels no one wants to talk about. But we'll get to that later.)

The last sewer tour was long since done for the night and the entrance was bolted shut (there went 24 euros for unused tickets), but Sylvie twisted the numbers on a combination lock with practiced ease.

"This is a side entrance," she said. "My grandfather is one of the engineers who maintain the tunnels used for tours. It is because of him that I knew of the perfect hiding place."

They stepped inside and immediately noticed the aroma. Yes, let's go with the word *aroma*. It's much more genteel than *stink*.

"The light switch is on this wall." There was the sound of Sylvie scrabbling at the brick and a loud snap, and light flooded the space. It was a tunnel, arched, made of limestone. There were pipes running along one wall, four or five of them in different sizes.

And the aroma.

"This way," Sylvie said, and led them onto a steel catwalk. The catwalk took a hard right turn away from the pipes and into a place that smelled less but seemed older. Here the brick was weathered and crumbly.

"This area is not safe for tours," Sylvie explained.

"Then why is it safe for us?" Dietmar wondered.

"It isn't. But it leads to our hiding place."

The tunnel had begun to narrow. Already a tall man would not have been able to walk erect. They reached the end of the reassuring catwalk and had to step down onto damp, worn stones that formed a walkway beside the channel.

There was no question that in a hard rain the two feet of sludgy, smelly water running through the channel would swell to fill half this tunnel and become a raging white-brown river.

"Not much farther," Sylvie said.

Only now there were no longer lights running down the roof of the chamber. It was getting darker, and ahead was absolute darkness.

"I should have picked up a flashlight!" Sylvie cried. "I was shaken up; I forgot."

"Phones will do the trick," Jarrah said. She whipped out her phone, pushed a button, and shone an amazingly dim and pitiful light at the darkness ahead.

The others all did the same so that it was six dim,

pitiful lights combining to make one dim, pitiful light. But it was enough to let them place their feet carefully, one before the other.

"It's not that much farther," Sylvie said.

But it was that much farther. Soon they lost sight of the lit part of the sewer. Now they were a tiny island of dim light shuffling along while they all tried really hard not to think about rats.

Because once you start thinking about rats, well, there's no unthinking it, is there?

Rats.

And in Mack's case, claustrophobia. Darkness in an underground space is one of the starting points for serious claustrophobia. After all, claustrophobia is a fear of small, enclosed spaces, which is to say, caskets, which is to say, being buried alive, which was not so very different from being twenty feet down in a musty sewer in the dark.

"Mmm-hhhh-nnn," Mack moaned without realizing it.

What goes really badly with being buried alive?

Rats.

And something out there in the dark was making

scritchy-scratchy little noises.

Scritchy.

"Mmmm-rrrr-nnnhhh!" Mack said more urgently.

Stefan clamped a hand over his mouth about a milli-second before Mack was going to let go with a moan that turned into a kind of trilling scream.

"Mmmph!" Mack said.

"Yeah," Stefan answered.

In a matter of seconds Mack was going to start squirming and thrashing. If necessary, Stefan would punch him in the head and either stun him or knock him unconscious. Neither was a great choice from Mack's point of view.

"Here," Sylvie said. They stopped, and in the sudden, profound quiet—the quiet of the grave, if I may—they could hear the sound of slow-moving sewer water and, ever more clearly, the sounds of rats.

Sylvie aimed her phone light at the wall. There was a slot. She stuck her hand in. And pulled on an iron lever within.

Suddenly bright light formed a tall rectangle.

"It's me, Sylvie," she said into the light.

And the rectangle grew until it was revealed as a

doorway. They stepped into a room with tall stone walls. Also, a flat-screen TV mounted on one of those walls. It was showing an old *Fairly OddParents* cartoon. But everyone was speaking French. Even Timmy.

Two kids stood within that room, eyes wary, poised to fight or flee.

One was a tall, painfully thin boy with brown hair and a sharp-featured, handsome face. He wore stylish glasses and had the collar of his shirt turned perfectly to frame his jawline.

The other boy was shorter, a bit stout, with full lips and a look of interested but sarcastic intelligence about him.

"We weren't really watching that," Rodrigo said, pointing his male-model chin at the TV.

"Actually, we were," Charlie said. "Because we only get the one channel down here. And no one thought to set the place up with books or games, so we're going slowly out of our minds and we would watch anything, anything at all."

"Except *Jersey Shore*," Rodrigo interjected. "I'll turn it off."

"No!" Mack said, way too urgently. "No, no. It's . . . soothing."

Obviously Stefan had let go of Mack. Stefan had a pretty good grasp of Mack's phobias by this point. He wasn't academically gifted, Stefan, but he had a certain intuitive grasp of other people's weaknesses. He got Mack. And so he knew that a well-lit underground room, especially one with a TV, was manageable for Mack. After all, no one ever got buried alive with a TV and Nicktoons playing.

Sylvie did the formal introductions. And she gave a brief explanation. "Long ago this was a secret place for people hiding from the king."

"Which king?"

"All of them, really. All of them tried to kill their enemies." Sylvie shrugged. "Kings. It's what they do. Later they hid from the emperors. And various invaders. Most recently cheese makers have used it to hide from health inspectors from Brussels. And now, we use it."

"How did you know you had to hide?" Mack asked, feeling the panic sweat begin to cool.

"A creature that fires tiny arrows out of its fingers shot me once here." Rodrigo pointed to his left bicep.

"And would have shot me many more places except that I jumped out of a second-floor window."

"I wonder if those are Bowands," Mack said wearily. He hadn't seen them, just heard of them in one of Grimluk's grim perorations.[32]

"And I figured it out when an old fart dressed in green sicced a bunch of lederhosen-wearing dwarves on me," Charlie said.

"Paddy 'Nine Iron' Trout and the treasonous Tong Elves," Jarrah said.

"What's that, a rock band?" Charlie asked.

"A Nafia assassin and . . . well, a bunch of treasonous Tong Elves."

"Okay then, it's all perfectly clear," Charlie said sarcastically. "Can we get out of here now? I doubt you've noticed, but it smells a bit down here. And the entertainment options are quite limited."

"Things are a little dangerous out there," Mack said. "So we need to be prepared. Let's take a minute and plan."

"I've got it," Charlie said. "You stay and plan; I am out of here."

---

32 That's right: perorations. Drop that word on your teacher someday. Instant A+.

"Dude," Mack said, and put his hand on the boy's arm.

Charlie's eyes narrowed dangerously. "Hey. Who died and made you king?"

"He's the leader of the group," Jarrah said, looking every bit as dangerous as Charlie.

"Says who?" Charlie demanded.

"Says Grimluk," Mack said.

"And the rest of us," Jarrah said.

"And me," Stefan said.

Then Charlie had an opportunity to take a close-up look at Stefan because Stefan stepped up to him and stood very close, which brought Charlie's nose to about the level of Stefan's muscle-bound chest and swollen biceps.

"Yes, well, all right then," Charlie said briskly.

Mack sat down on the couch. He sighed. "We're trapped in this game where we're trying to get the Twelve together and Risky is chasing us. All she has to do to win is make sure we never get to twelve. And she already has Valin. So, I've been thinking about this—in between being stomped by giants—and I think we need to go on the offensive. We need to start hitting back now that we have the Key. Maybe the first thing to do is go right at them."

"Go at them?" Dietmar asked in a shrill, disbelieving voice. "How do we do that?"

Mack shrugged. He hadn't figured that out yet.

"If I want a fight, I call someone out," Stefan said.

"What does that mean, call someone out?" Rodrigo asked, intrigued, as if he liked the sound of it.

"It means I say, 'You, me, after school,'" Stefan said.

Mack had received just such an invitation from Stefan. So had many others. Stefan had changed, but he had not changed completely.

"We issue a challenge? Why would we do that?" Dietmar asked.

"To throw them off balance," Xiao said. "To force them out into the open. For all the power of my people, we have survived by remaining hidden. The dragons of China would never have survived if people had known about us."

"Maybe that's the takeaway from old Billy Blisterthöng, eh?" Jarrah said, nodding. "He was all tough and bad so long as he was invisible to the world."

Sylvie said, "People have seen the YouTubes of

different things you have done, but I have read the comments and most people think they are fake. Many think they are some strange advertising, as if the display of your raw emotions and the suspension of normalcy is too threatening to accept. They prefer the comfort of self-deception. It is as if to believe this truth is to be cast into the abyss, the bottomless emptiness that is existence without—"

"Riiight," Jarrah said, cutting her off with a sigh and rolling her eyes. "We gotta make people believe us. Gotta rub their faces in it."

Mack nodded. "We need help. Which means we need people looking for the Skirrit and the Tong Elves and the Gudridan. We need people to be watching for Paddy Nine Iron. And Valin."

"Call them out," Charlie said, adopting the phrase. Then, in a sardonic tone, "What could possibly go wrong?"

Mack pulled out the two pieces of the Key and laid them on the coffee table.

"We prepared a little and still ended up nearly getting killed by those giant things. We need more. We need each of us to know at least three spells in

Vargran. We need some of those to be things we do on our own, and others to be things we can do together, in combinations."

Xiao sat down beside him and gazed thoughtfully at the stone circles. "There are not a lot of words in this language. We should be able to learn a fair amount. But where do we start?"

Mack thought about that, as did the others. Then he smiled. "We want something very big and very public. Something undeniable, right? Okay, then simple question: What's the Vargran word for 'tower'?"

Twenty-two

They worked the night through, not that it was ever daylight down in the sewer tunnels.

But by morning they were a tighter group than they had been. They were prepared. They had a plan. Well, a plan of sorts.

But there's an old saying among soldiers: no plan ever survives contact with the enemy.

Contact with the enemy came much sooner than they had expected.

As they were retracing their steps toward the

lighted part of the tunnel, Mack again heard the scritchy-scratchy sound of rats. Stefan was walking right behind him, prepared for a friendly mouth clamp and possible head smack.

Mack felt a little better walking out of the sewers than he had walking in, for the same reason it's better to be getting out of a casket than into one.

He had it under control, so long as they didn't stay down there too long. And so long as there weren't, oh, let's say, rats.

Mack had picked up a pretty good flashlight in the underground hideaway, so he now aimed it at the rats, hoping to scare them off.

Only they were not rats. Not even big rats. They were, for lack of a better word, centipedes.

Big centipedes.

The flashlight beam highlighted a particular one that was just a little bit out in front of the others. Mack stared for what felt like a very long time but was probably no more than a second. In that second he saw a glistening, pulsating, yellow-white wormlike body, way too many legs, and a face dominated by dead-staring insect eyes and gnashing mouthparts, and really, that was all he needed to know to figure out his next statement. Which was:

"Ruuuuun!"

The others had seen what he'd seen and, not surprisingly, they agreed with his recommendation that they ruuuuun!

They ran. But so did the centipede things. And with that many legs, they were fast. They were especially fast running upside down on the ceiling. Something about six-foot-long insects running down the arched roof of an ancient sewer struck particular terror into Mack, and he wondered in some still-functioning part of his mind whether he had just developed a phobia about centipedes.

But no: phobias are irrational fears, and this fear was extremely rational because now one of the creatures was directly over Mack's head. He could reach up and touch it. (He didn't.)

But there was Stefan, right beside Mack. He pushed Mack forward, then leaped straight up, wrapped his arms around the giant bug, and yanked it down off the ceiling.

The centipede landed on its back, legs motoring

madly in the air as it squirmed and tried to turn over. Stefan stomped once. Hard. His foot landed right where a centipede might have a neck if it had one (no, it didn't), and two segments of the creature's body popped apart. Thick, viscous yellow goo, like Play-Doh pushed through one of those squishy machines, came fast then slowed.

The centipede's tail end thrashed. The mouthparts gnashed.

Stefan looked at the hundreds of bugs now coating every surface of the sewer tunnel and said, "Who's next?"

The bug army had stopped to witness the one-sided combat. Now they seemed uncertain whether to rush Stefan or not. So Stefan helped them make up their minds. He squatted beside the squashed bug and twisted until its head came all the way off. Through all this, the mouthparts, driven by the simple bug nervous system, continued to gnash.

Stefan stood up, held the head with the gnashing mouthparts out like a weapon. And laughed.

The centipedes were creatures of the Pale Queen. And they lived beneath Paris (and a few other cities as well), so they'd seen some things down through the ages. But they had not seen an apparently crazy teenager brandishing the head of their squashed leader.

Regular centipedes are not known to have a reverse gear.

These did.

The centipede army backed slowly away, reversing down the tunnel.

Stefan looked at Mack, showed him the head, and said, "Can I keep this?"

"Sure," Mack said. "As long as you carry it."

Stefan stuck the head under his arm, much as a Frenchman might carry a baguette, and they marched, unhurried, toward the lit areas of the sewers and, hopefully, safety.

Rodrigo was next to Mack. "You know, I wondered what Stefan's purpose was. I think I understand perfectly now." He walked a few more steps. "And I think I am just the smallest bit afraid of him."

Mack shrugged. "He's much better to have on your side than against you."

They emerged at last into the too-bright light of a beautiful Parisian day. After the dimness below, they blinked and shaded their eyes for a while.

"So, the Eiffel Tower is that way," Dietmar said, pointing downriver. "Not so far. We can take a Métro or—"

"I think I've seen enough of underground Paris," Charlie said. "I'm supposed to be here on a school tour. And I must say, this is the worst tour ever."

"Let's walk along the river," Sylvie suggested.

"Should we cross back to the other side?" Xiao wondered.

"Over the same bridge with those giant things?" Dietmar said. "That seems like a bad idea."

So they walked along in lovely fall sunlight next to the Seine. It was almost possible to forget the deadly nature of their mission. There are some good things about being twelve years old: you recover quickly from events that might destroy the mind and break the will of an adult. Adults are fragile and easily frightened. Try saying the word *biopsy* to an adult. Or *tax audit*. See? It's easy to scare an adult.

But the effects of sunlight and the slow-moving river and the amazing beauty of the city around them restored their spirits more quickly than an adult could even imagine. The only off note was that some of the people they passed stared at Stefan's giant bug head, which was now gnashing more feebly, but still gnashing.

Mack pulled out his phone to check for messages. There were about a dozen, including various spams, something from his school, two Facebook friend requests, and something from the golem.

He sighed. No, he was feeling good finally. It was not time to hear that the golem had burned down the house or whatever. Later.

They reached a pedestrian bridge. It was a sturdy thing, quite capable of carrying a car or two, but strictly for pedestrians. They crossed here, thinking it appeared giant-free. And from the middle of the bridge they could see the tower in all its magnificence. Not very near, but not very far, either.

They paused there for a moment for Stefan to throw the centipede head into the river. "It stopped moving," he explained ruefully. "It was only cool as long as it was moving."

A long *bateau mouche* was coming toward them, and a tugboat was chugging by below, going the other way. They watched the boats and therefore missed seeing the police car that pulled up very abruptly at the far end of the bridge.

Two blue-uniformed officers stepped out. More police cars arrived. More cops. Or flics, as the French would say.

Jarrah was the first to spot trouble. "Uh-oh," she said.

There were now close to a dozen cops.

Mack shot an anxious look back the way they had come. A big police van had just pulled up, and guys in body armor carrying plastic shields were piling out in a very professional way.

"I can use the disappearing spell on them," Jarrah said.

"No," Xiao said quickly. "They are the legitimate forces of law and order."

This brought a raised eyebrow from Jarrah, a snort of disbelief from Charlie, a sage head nod from Dietmar, and a shrug from Sylvie.

Mack said, "Xiao's right. We don't hurt the good guys. Let's try talking to them."

He stepped to the middle of the Passerelle Debilly.

He held his hands out, palms open, and smiled. The intent was to show he was harmless and not looking for trouble.

But some things translate better than others in foreign lands. The palms and the open arms were fine. But Parisians have a different attitude toward smiles than Americans do. So to the flics, this looked mighty suspicious.

A plainclothes officer, a woman with dark hair and a no-nonsense attitude, pushed through the uniforms. "You must come with us," she said in firm but charmingly accented English.

"Sorry, ma'am, we can't do that," Mack said.

"But I insist," the woman said. "We know that you were involved in the disturbing incidents on the bridge. People were hurt."

"Sorry about that. But we're kind of in the middle of something," Mack said. Again in his most winning, charming, harmless, trustworthy, smiling way.

"I am Inspecteur Bonnard of the police nationale," she said. It wasn't in the nature of a friendly introduction. "You will come peacefully. Or you will come with . . . difficulty. But either way, you will come."

"Boat," Stefan said. Just that one word. And his eyes flicked toward the *bateau mouche* that was passing beneath them.

"We'll get killed," Mack hissed, still smiling at the *inspecteur* in an ingratiating way that really wasn't working.

"Nah," Jarrah said dismissively. "We'll most likely survive."

"I will count to three," the *inspecteur* said. "I will not count slowly."

"Oy," Mack said, and sighed. "Everyone? Follow me."

He turned suddenly and raced for the railing on the far side of the bridge. The police were not slow to notice. From both sides the uniforms surged.

Mack jumped, landed on the rail, and leaped.

Twenty-three

Now, if this were a movie, we'd know exactly what happens next. The Magnifica plus Stefan would leap and then fall in slow motion while yelling comical catchphrases. They would land on the *bateau mouche*'s awning and slide down safely, and the cops would be left fuming helplessly.

Ah, if only life could be a movie. Or a movie could be life. Although not some movies.

As it happened, Mack did not land on an awning; he landed on a transparent covering that looked like it might be glass but was in fact plastic. The plastic didn't break. It cracked from the impact but it was thick and strong, so it didn't shatter. Mack landed hard on his heels, fell on his butt, smacked his head, and lay as stunned as a slapped catfish.[33]

Sylvie, Xiao, and Charlie all landed in a heap of tangled legs and arms. The two girls seemed to have landed on top of Charlie, who softened their landing but was now groaning that his back was broken. (It wasn't.)

Jarrah was the only one to shout anything at all, and it was, "Yeeeeeaaaah!" followed shortly by, "Owww, that hurt." Followed by some interesting Australian expressions that we cannot repeat here lest some Australian get hold of this book and be offended.

Dietmar missed the boat altogether and landed in the water. So did Rodrigo.

However they both landed quite close to the side of the *bateau*, and when Stefan leaped last and spotted their splashes, he hit the plastic cover, bounced easily off the side into the water, and came up with one Rodrigo and one Dietmar in each hand.

---

33. Yes, that's absolutely a saying. What, you've never heard *stunned as a slapped catfish*? Well, now you have.

He basically threw Dietmar aboard. Then he grabbed one of the bumpers, held on, and pushed Rodrigo up over the side before following him up.

The police refused to be comically helpless. Instead they hopped into their vehicles and were now, with sirens lamenting loudly and blue lights flashing, racing down both banks of the Seine.

Also, in a movie the crew of the boat would just kind of shrug off the fact that eight kids had dropped onto their boat from a bridge. But in reality they were somewhat upset, actually. The dropping bodies had made a mess of the plastic, and the passengers were concerned and asking questions like, "Is this normal?" and, "Is this part of some kind of street theater?" And one man even asked, "Are they mimes?"

The French are very touchy on the subject of mimes, so this created some real resentment on the part of the crew. Said crew were now edging forward cautiously and demanding to know just who they thought they were landing like that without even a ticket. One of the crew was holding a pepper mill as a weapon.

Mack reached for his pocket.

The armed crewman said, "Don't try anything!"

"I'm just reaching for a credit card," Mack said. And out came the black plastic rectangle that signaled great wealth. "I want to pay for tickets, and I'll pay for damages. And I'd like to leave a tip of five hundred euros for every crew member and twice that for the captain!"

There was a sudden mood change. The pepper mill disappeared, a credit card reader appeared in its place, and someone brought bandages for Jarrah's scraped leg and foot.

"We're heading the wrong direction," Dietmar pointed out. "The Eiffel Tower is the other way."

"Yeah," Mack agreed. "And the cops are keeping up with us."

The crew now brought them café au lait and hot chocolate and the most perfect croissants, along with pots of preserves and tubs of butter. The *bateau* churned along at a good speed—just fast enough that the cops couldn't catch up by the time they reached Pont de l'Alma again.

The cops made pretty good progress after that and almost got onto the next bridge, but not quite. Then it seemed the police were slowed by traffic and the *bateau* might get away altogether.

"We might just make it," Rodrigo said.

"Bet you a fiver we don't," Charlie said, holding out his hand for Rodrigo to shake on the bet.

As they rounded a bend, up loomed an island, and on that island was the huge Gothic church called Notre-Dame, with its spires visible despite being at the far end.

The river narrowed. Police boats waited like sharks for a guppy.

The captain sent his apologies and said that he was bound to obey the police boats. It was one thing to pretend not to see police cars racing frantically to catch up. This was a whole different kettle of fish. These were boats.

The police cars had reached the Pont Neuf ahead of them as well, so it was more or less the entire Paris police force arrayed along the bridge or in boats just in front of the bridge.

"My compliments to the captain," Mack said, because he'd seen that in a movie once, "and tell him we understand."

"What do we do now?" Dietmar asked.

Mack stifled an urge to say a sarcastic, Oh, now you want me to make the decisions.

They were trapped. The boat couldn't turn around even if the captain had wanted to. Either they fought the police, or they would have to be able to walk on water.

Which is not something that is done on a regular basis.

"I have a crazy idea," Mack said.

"Let's do it!" Jarrah and Stefan both said.

"You haven't even heard what it is yet!" Xiao protested.

Jarrah shrugged. "He said it was crazy"—as though that was enough.

"We know the Vargran for 'water.' And we know the Vargran word for 'walk,'" Mack said. He just let that hang there in the air for a minute as the others stared at him.

"Are you out of your mind?" Charlie demanded at

last, and it was pretty clear that Sylvie, Rodrigo, and Xiao shared this opinion.

Surprisingly, it was Dietmar who said, "Very clever. Ingenious. If it works."

"It feels big," Xiao said. "Like it would take all of us together."

"And would it work for Stefan?" Rodrigo asked.

"If it works for us and not him, we drag him along," Mack said.

"And if it doesn't work at all, we end up wet and cold and looking ridiculous!" Charlie said.

Mack ignored him. "Rodrigo and Jarrah, you haul Stefan if necessary. We head down the right side of the island, where the river is narrowest—the cop boats aren't over on that side. We get out of sight of the boats and the bridges and then we head up into the city and try to disappear."

Jarrah grinned and grabbed Charlie's hand, shook it firmly, and said, "Welcome to the Magnificent Twelve, mate."

The boat slowed, and the police boats were just thirty feet away when together the Magnifica spoke the words *booj-il ebway truk (sniff)oh* with a certain fervent energy.

Then Mack vaulted over the side.

His feet landed on water. His knees buckled. But he did not sink. The water was not dry and it was not suddenly flat or solid or unmoving. In fact, his shoes were wet immediately. They seemed to sink an inch or two with each step, and tiny waves splashed over his ankles. But he did not sink.

"Okay, I did not expect that to work," Mack said. He looked back to see the others gaping at him. "Come on," he urged, with far more confidence than he felt. "No problem."

They jumped.

Stefan plunged.

Rodrigo and Jarrah grabbed an arm each and hauled him after them as they ran in a soggy, shuffling way. It was a very odd thing to watch: two running on water, dragging a third like he was a fallen water-skier.

The current was against them, so they couldn't run as fast as they might have liked—it was a bit like running in the wrong direction on a treadmill. But the mere fact that they were running at all on water seemed to have finally caused the cops to stop and gape in frozen astonishment.

The kids raced down the narrow part of the river, island on their left, the Left Bank on their right, and passed beneath a series of very low, mossy-bottomed bridges. Soon they were in the shadow of the great cathedral.

And there at last, just as they were feeling pretty good about themselves, and Mack was congratulating himself on his out-of-the-box thinking, they saw a figure standing on the last bridge, the one that led directly from the Left Bank to Notre-Dame.

He was a boy, clearly, although dressed a bit flamboyantly in puffy maroon pantaloons and a tight yellow vest over a full-cut white shirt. He wore a sword at his side.

Yes: a sword.

In addition to the sword, Mack spotted nunchakus stuffed into his belt. And some kind of wickedly curved knife on the other side.

"My half brother," Sylvie hissed.

It was indeed Valin. He was smirking at them, nodding appreciatively, and when they stopped to stare up at him, he did an ironic slow clap.

"Very nice, Mack," Valin said.

"Valin! Join us," Mack said.

Jarrah and Rodrigo dragged the soggy Stefan up beside Mack.

"He's just one guy," Jarrah said.

"He's one guy we can't hurt," Mack said through gritted teeth. "Don't forget: we need him."

"I don't think I would have thought of walking on water," Valin called down. "That is very clever."

"Valin, you have to join us," Mack insisted, despite the ridiculousness of pleading up at him while standing on a river.

"Join you?" Valin spat. "Join the scion of a family that did terrible injustice to my ancestors? Never!"

"I don't even know what you're talking about," Mack pleaded.

"If I were you, Sylvie," Valin said, "I would join with me, instead. You're being a fool. You can never defeat the Pale Queen. Don't you know that even now, as her time approaches, her power grows? Don't you know that her power flows through me? Fools! You have Vargran, yes, but so do I. And I have the power of Her Majesty as well!"

"I will not join you, Valin," Sylvie said stoutly. "And if you serve her, it will mean that someday you must kill me."

That actually brought evidence of a twinge of conscience to Valin's face. He drew back just a little. But then he seemed to shake it off. "That is your choice, Sylvie *cherie.* And it will be your doom."

Then he began to chant Vargran words. He raised his hands high, and the sky, the pure blue sky, began to fill with boiling dark clouds.

From those swirling, malevolent clouds a lightning bolt stabbed through the sudden eerie darkness. It struck the cathedral.

Mack looked instinctively at the beautiful old stonework, expecting to see damage.

Rows of gargoyles stared down with hideous malevolence. (Medieval church builders loved them some gargoyles.)

Then, the gargoyle that had taken the main blast of the lightning bolt . . . blinked.

If you read about the gargoyles of Notre-Dame, you may come across a story that they were mostly used to direct rainwater. This is nonsense, of course. Okay, not total nonsense because they were used to keep the rain that rushes down off the roof from draining down the side of the church and messing up the nice stonework.

But that doesn't explain why they look like demons. There are dozens of other ways to design a rainspout. They could have been just pipes. Or Hello Kitties. But no, they were carved to look like demons—bits of hungry lion and screeching eagle and sinister wolf and dragon.

Gargoyles were there to send a message to people—people who, in the Middle Ages, mostly couldn't read. The message was that the end of the world was nigh and they'd better show up for service on Sunday. Or else.

These particular gargoyles were very old, eroded stone figures, so they'd lost some of their fearsomeness. Unless of course you woke them up with a magic spell and a bolt of lightning, because then, well, then they got very real, very fast, and in very lifelike detail.

"That thing just eyeballed me," Stefan said.

"Yep," Mack agreed.

"Fly, my gargoyles, fly!" Valin cackled madly, arms upraised. "Destroy them. Destroy them all!"

Needless to say, he added a crazy laugh that went, "Ahhh-ha-ha-ha-haaaahhhh!"

The lightning-struck gargoyle grew detailed. Long years had worn away the scales, and roughened the edges of its wings, and dulled the sharpness of its talons. Now those emerged from the stone. They became whole and complete and terrifying.

This was no longer a stone sculpture to frighten children. It was a living, steam-breathing emissary of hell.

The gargoyle then emitted a cry. How to describe it? A cry full of furious frustration, sudden unexpected liberation, and a realization that all its centuries of imprisonment as a stone object, all its forced immobility and helplessness, were at an end.

The gargoyle opened its leathery wings, fixed its mad eyes on Mack, and swooped down from its roofline perch.

Others then moved. Others then stared with fixed hatred on the small band of kids standing (rather improbably) in the middle of the Seine.

Dozens?

No, more than dozens. Hundreds!

226

Some had only half a body—they had been sculpted that way. Some leered lasciviously while others glared furiously. Some had wings; some moved sinuously like snakes through the air. They seemed almost to swim down out of a sky boiling gray and black and riven by bolts of lightning.

"We don't want to go that way anyhow," Mack yelled. "Back! Back!"

They turned and ran across the water. Now the current was their friend. Each step was like a step and a half. It was strangely like ice-skating somehow, but dragging Stefan through the water was slowing them down.

The first gargoyle raked Mack's hair with its talons. Blood dribbled down his face and he made a sort of frightened whinnying sound, like a horse that's just seen a rattlesnake.

They passed beneath the first small bridge, a temporary—very temporary—respite, then out the other side for a renewed onslaught.

But at the same time his mind was working furiously. He had Vargran. They all did. But the *enlightened puissance* was an easily exhausted resource: like the patience of a boy who finds himself in a Claire's store, or a girl who finds herself in a discussion of belching, or a reader forced to wade through an overly long simile.

The point is, the *enlightened puissance* is like a battery that runs down and then needs to be recharged. So Mack had to take that into account. He'd already used up a whole lot of *e.p.* walking on water. And they would need all their combined strength to pull off the dramatic stunt they were planning.

On the other hand, it was important not to die.

Beneath the next bridge and out, and beneath and out, and this time the gargoyles encircled them, swooping to cut them off so that they had to push and flail and bat at monsters to get out the other side.

"We must use the Vargran!" Rodrigo cried seconds before a gargoyle struck him in the back and knocked him forward. Rodrigo hit the water, but instead of landing on it as though it was solid, he plunged in, bellyflop-style. He bobbed up after a second, but in order to walk on the water, he needed first to be able to walk.

Sylvie, Charlie, and Xiao grabbed Rodrigo's arms

and hauled him up, up until he could get one foot above the surface. Then he was able to stand. But pulling this off had made the knot of four kids a focus for the gargoyles. They swarmed in a fast-moving spiral, all gray talons and beaks, horns and wings.

"Stefan!" Mack yelled. "Swim for the bridge on your own. Dietmar and Jarrah with me!"

He led them in a body slam against the spinning gargoyles. But that so didn't work. Dietmar was knocked down into the water, just like Rodrigo had been. A gargoyle had talons in Jarrah's hair and was dragging her, pulling her away.

Blam!

Something hit the leonine creature that had Jarrah by the hair.

Blam! Blam!

Mack turned in amazement and saw that the current had carried them closer to the big bridge than he had realized. The bridge where the cops were waiting. It was police marksmen shooting at the gargoyles.

The bullets would only have chipped the stone of a regular gargoyle. But these were living creatures now, however bizarre and unnatural. The bullets struck home and brought forth cries of pain and outrage. Black blood boiled up through skin the color of cement.

"Run! Run!" Mack cried, and windmilled his arm to show the way. "We have to get past the bridge!"

The gargoyles had hesitated and allowed just enough time for the group to haul Dietmar onto dry water, where they were running flat-out now. Valin's voice still reached them, far-off but shrill and determined.

"Attack!" he cried. "Attack!"

The hesitant gargoyles had no choice but to obey.

Here is the scene so that you have it clear in your mind:

Seven kids running on gray-blue water as if it was some sort of soggy playing field.

One boy in the water, swimming with powerful strokes even as his friends caught up to him.

The famous Pont Neuf, a series of stone arches, beautifully proportioned, stark and white and built to look a bit like the wall of an old castle. And atop that bridge an array of flashing lights, blue uniforms, body armor, and pointed guns.

Police boats, a mismatched collection, some like simple cabin cruisers of the sort you'd see in any marina, others black-hulled and blunt-snouted like converted barges. And a few very small, fast boats with men in scuba suits.

Gargoyles, a dark cloud of them, diving on the racing Magnifica.

"*Tirez!*" the *inspecteur* cried, and a volley of shots rang out. Then the firing went on, ragged but continuous. The noise was unbelievable, but the effect was welcome. Gargoyles died in the air, turned to stone again, and plunged into the Seine like a rain of boulders.

Mack and the rest ran beneath the Pont Neuf, out the other side, past the straggling police boats that were now rushing to join the battle of flic vs. gargoyle.

The battered, bruised, wet, and terrified group clambered aboard a passing barge that was hauling a load of sand.

The owner-captain yelled and protested until Sylvie explained in weary French that these eight had escaped from the terror upstream, and that they were also running from *les flics.*

This engaged the man's sympathies and he hid them in his small, homey cabin until they were alongside the Eiffel Tower.

"Okay," Mack said, exhausted. "Now we tell the world. And we make the world listen."

Twenty-four

MEANWHILE, BACK AT RICHARD GERE
MIDDLE SCHOOL[34]

"It's today," Camaro Angianelli said, punching the golem in the shoulder. It was an affectionate punch. It would have affectionately given a huge affectionate bruise to anyone else, but Camaro had long since realized that the golem was pretty much impervious to bruising.

---

34 Yes, they're still Pupfish and they're still Fighting.

"Yes, it is today," the golem replied. In fact it was always today. It was never yesterday or tomorrow, it was always today. The golem had noticed this.

"Will you be there?" Camaro asked.

This felt like it might be a bit of a trick question. The golem had never been anywhere but "here," just as it was always "today."

"Where?" the golem asked cautiously. They were in the hallway, standing next to the golem's locker. The locker contained his schoolbooks, several twigs, a plastic trash can full of moist mud—just in case he did end up taking a shower—and a sketch he had drawn of Grimluk and taped to the inside of the door. The sketch wasn't very good—it was recognizably Grimluk, but it lacked perspective.

"What is that?" Camaro demanded, noticing the portrait for the first time. "Is that your grandpa?"

"That is Grimluk, my creator," Mack said.

Camaro frowned. "God? God's looking like he needs dental work. No offense. Anyway, you'll be there, right? You said you would."

Well, there she had him. He must have said he would. Now he just had to remember what he'd said he would do. And where. Asking why would probably be greedy.

"Yes. I will be . . ." At this he hesitated. Because he had never been anywhere other than "here" and indeed didn't see how it was possible to be "there."

"The usual place," Camaro said helpfully.

"Ah."

"Me and Tony Pooch. All you have to do is watch my back."

"You have a flat back."

"Are you insulting my back?"

"No. I like watching your back. I see it whenever you walk away."

Camaro narrowed her eyes, suspicious that this was an obscure insult. "Just be there," she said, and showed him her back as she walked away.

The golem checked his phone. Still nothing from Mack. It was worrying him, and worry was a very new emotion for him. He didn't know how much of it to do at a single stretch. Was it good to worry constantly? Or should he pick a time or place and worry really hard, then stop?

One of the things that worried him was that he

had, in addition to his own phone, brought Risky's phone with him to school. It was in his pocket. He had intended to either leave it home or smash it with the dining room table, but he had found he couldn't quite bring himself to do either.

And now it was in his pocket. Waiting to ring.

"I don't know how to worry," he said to the portrait of Grimluk. "You didn't teach me that."

WWMD? What would Mack do?

Slowly he drew out both phones. The one that came from Risky. The one that led to Mack.

Still no response from Mack.

He had been told—in very definite terms—not to call Mack, only to text or email. That instruction came directly from Mack himself, which meant it was right.

Unless it wasn't.

That was a crazy thought. The golem laughed.

But what if it was possible? What if Mack . . . was wrong?

The golem hit the home button, slid the bar aside, and punched in his password: 1111.[35]

---

35 Don't tell anyone: it's a secret.

Twenty-five

The Eiffel Tower.

It's big. Especially when you're right up under it, which is where our wet, bloodied, scratched, scarred, scared, and very determined little band was.

There are four big legs to the tower. Each is planted on a massive concrete pedestal. Around each pedestal are the ticket booths, a place where you can buy snacks, the base of the elevator, and a lot of people craning their necks to look up.

The tower is built out of millions of individual

pieces. It's not like they molded it all out of a single block of steel—you see each and every piece, every crossbar, every strut, every beam—15,000 pieces. And you see the fat rivets used to hold each piece in place. It's as if it were built entirely out of Popsicle sticks—if Popsicle sticks were iron and coated with thick gray-brown paint. But from a little distance it appears very delicate, as if it were made out of lace.

There are three decks on the Eiffel Tower. The first one is about a quarter of the way up. A second deck is closer to the halfway point. And the very top, *le tip top*, is 990 feet up there. Way up.

There's an elevator connecting the three decks. There are also stairs to the lowest two decks.

The whole thing is placed plop beside the river Seine, at one end of a long, rectangular field called the Champ de Mars, or the Field of Mars. Because the French love them some Mars bars.[36]

"Let's take the elevator," Mack said wearily. "I don't think I could handle stairs."

Easier said than done. There was a line, and tickets had to be purchased, and then another line. Finally

---

36 This may not be 100 percent true.

the elevator, which, in keeping with the whole Eiffel Tower look, was an open iron cage sort of thing. It rose at an angle as it swept up the arc of the tower's leg, and straightened as the tower straightened.

Suddenly, as the iron-bound view of Paris widened, Mack was terribly homesick. He missed his parents. He missed his room. He missed his school. He even missed the kids at school. And he almost missed some of his teachers.

He hadn't wanted to look at any pictures from home because they would make him sad. But now he was weary to the point where sad would be a real improvement. He pulled out his phone and opened his personal photos. Pictures of kids at school. Pictures for some reason of the school bus. A picture of his parents playing volleyball at some beach somewhere some long, long time ago.

He tapped on his messages. The golem, of course. Mack almost didn't open it.

Then he did.

I'm afraid. A girl named Risky was here. I think she will make me hurt people. Your golem. >:-(

Mack stopped breathing.

"Are we getting off here?" Xiao asked.

The elevator had come to a stop, and many of the people were exiting. It was the first level.

"Is this it?" Charlie prodded when Mack didn't answer.

Risky. She had been there. In his home. In his actual home!

I think she will make me hurt people.

"Let's go on up to the second floor," Jarrah said, speaking for Mack.

It had always been possible, Mack knew. Sooner or later they would go for his family. After all, Paddy "Nine Iron" Trout had already tried by shoving snakes in through the window of Mack's house.

But Mack had hoped that when he left Sedona they would go after him and him alone. Not his family.

He swallowed, but his mouth was dry.

Could the golem be made to hurt people? The golem was a sweet goof, not some kind of monster.

But Mack's logical brain argued back: *No, he's whatever he's made to be.*

240

And his logical brain was also replaying Risky's offer. Join her. Join her now and his family, maybe his whole town, would be safe.

Other families . . . Other towns . . .

"You okay, mate?" Jarrah asked him.

What had he thought? That this was all a game and that no one would get hurt? Had he imagined they'd leave his family alone? The Pale Queen would leave no one's family alone.

The elevator came to the second floor. Mack was swept along with the rest as they got out.

"Okay, now what?" Rodrigo asked.

"Mack." Xiao put her hand on his arm.

They were all staring at him. There was no putting off the decision. A decision that might doom his family.

"Text message," he said flatly. "Risky has been to my home. She got to my golem."

"What? That is intolerable!" Dietmar cried.

Mack liked him for that. The German boy's outrage was genuine.

"What do we do?" Charlie asked. And Mack liked that, too. *We.* What do we do?

Mack took a deep breath. "We—"

His phone rang. His phone never rang. But it rang now.

He saw the caller ID. It was the golem.

"Yeah," Mack said.

"Mack. It's me, your golem."

"I know. I got your text."

"Mack, I'm afraid. Risky has given me a second phone. I think she can use it to make me . . . to make me not 'Be Mack' but be something else."

"Listen to me: smash that phone she gave you."

"I . . . I tried, Mack."

"Smash it now, Golem. Smash it right now!"

"My hands won't. . . ."

Mack closed his eyes and fought down a wave of panic. "Where are you?"

"At school."

"Listen to me, Golem. Who can you trust there? Who can you go to? Who can help?"

The golem was silent for a minute. Mack waited, eyes closed, unwilling to meet the worried gaze of his friends.

The golem came up with a name.

Mack breathed. "Yeah, Golem. That's what you do. Right now!"

The line went dead.

"What must we do?" Sylvie asked.

With shaking fingers, Mack shoved his phone back into his pocket.

"We have a plan," Mack said softly. "We carry it out."

He walked on legs gone wobbly to the railing that looked down over the Champ de Mars. They were too high up for people down below to hear, but the kids had prepared for that.

"*Tine ovol ebway!*" Mack said in a loud, sure voice. In Vargran it meant, "Loud voice us." It was the best they could do with the clumsy ancient tongue. They could only hope the meaning was clear, or clear enough.

No worries, as Jarrah liked to say: once he had spoken the words, his voice was suddenly as loud as if he were talking through a bullhorn.

"People," he bellowed. "People down below. Cameras on!"

There were perhaps a hundred people down below

on the concrete and a few spreading out onto the grass, and they all looked. And those who had cameras turned them on.

"People of Earth!" he cried. "We are here to warn you of a terrible danger. The Pale Queen rises after three thousand years of captivity to enslave the human race!"

Suddenly Sylvie was translating his words into French, her voice only slightly less loud. Not that the French people below didn't understand the English— of course they did—but, being French, they would be insulted that someone was bellowing at them in English from their greatest national landmark.

"*Liberté, egalité, fraternité!*" Sylvie cried. "*En danger!*"

"We know you won't want to believe us," Mack cried. "We know you will need proof that magical and awful things are happening. So. We have arranged undeniable proof that nothing is like it was anymore."

In French Sylvie warned everyone to get back from the base of the tower. Absolutely no one obeyed.

"Let us hold hands," Xiao said, "and focus our power as one."

She took Mack's right hand. Dietmar took his left. Charlie beside Xiao, Jarrah with Dietmar, Sylvie and Rodrigo last.

"On one," Stefan said, conducting as agreed. "Three . . . two . . ."

Before he could say, "One!" the sky turned suddenly dark. A swirling cloud, almost a tornado, came down like a finger of doom.

"Is that us doing that?" Charlie yelled. "Because if it is, we should stop!"

"That's not our doing," Xiao said darkly. "I sense a great evil approaching."

"Then you should also sense me getting out of here," Charlie said. But he didn't move. He stayed. They all stayed and held hands.

The tornado touched down amid the crowd below, scattering hats and coats and handbags and cameras. People were knocked down like bowling pins. Dirt and debris flew.

Then, through the storm walked two figures. The wind did not touch them. The debris sailed harmlessly past them. An old, old man in green, waving a sword, scaring people away.

And beside him, a boy in ludicrous pirate gear, brandishing a curved blade.

Paddy "Nine Iron" Trout. And the traitor, Valin.

And from the sky, descending from the tornado's funnel, as if she were careening down a slide, came Risky.

She landed on the railing, stood there effortlessly, wearing a shimmery green dress that brought out the amazing green color of her eyes. Her red hair was a tornado all its own.

"Mack, Mack, Mack. I thought you understood: fun and games are over, Mack."

"Don't let her distract us!" Dietmar cried.

"Oh, shut up, Dirtmore," Risky said, and her right hand stretched as if it were putty. Stretched into a tentacle that reached for Dietmar's throat.

Stefan leaped, grabbed the tentacle, and was tossed aside with such force Mack feared he must have been killed.

"Together!" Mack cried. "NOW!"

And the ancient spell, the tongue of power, the words of magic were chanted in shrill, frightened, but absolutely unshakably determined voices.

"*Halk-ma exel azres!*"

Risky's pearly white movie-star teeth turned into the glittering daggers of a shark.

"Excuse me, just a moment, Mack: I have to send a message."

Twenty-six

MEANWHILE, AT RICHARD GERE MIDDLE SCHOOL[37]

The golem knew of only one person he could trust. He found her in social studies class, where she sat in the back row, lounging in her chair, with her booted feet propped on the shoulders of the kid sitting in front of her.

"Camaro!" the golem cried.

The teacher said, "Young man, do not interrupt

---

37 No! There's no time for that!

this . . ." And then the teacher realized who she was talking to, and who he was talking to, and decided whatever she had been about to say could wait. Indefinitely.

"T'sup, Mack?" Camaro asked.

"I need you. You're the only one I can trust."

Camaro was fourteen. (She was really very bright, smart even, but she had been held back. Mostly because the high school she should have been attending—Shirley MacLaine High—had begged the school not to promote her. In fact, they had given Richard Gere Middle School a much-needed copier and a utility van to keep her.)

In all her fourteen years, Camaro had never, ever, not even once, heard the words *I need you* aimed in her direction.

The words *you're the only one I can trust* brought tears to her eyes.

She took her feet off the shoulders of the boy in front of her.

She stood up.

She straightened her leather jacket.

She adjusted the metal-studded leather strap on her wrist.

And she said, "I'm your girl."

At that moment the phone buzzed. Slowly the golem pulled out his own phone.

Wrong phone. It was the other one that was buzzing.

His hand moved, as if of its own accord. It touched that terrible phone. Her phone.

"You have to stop me," the golem pleaded.

He opened the message.

And then, slowly, unstoppably, the golem slid the phone into his mouth.

His last semi-intelligible words were, "Shlop e, uh-maro!"

Twenty-seven

"*Halk-ma exel azres!*"

There was a cracking sound, like the earth itself was opening up. It was a sound like cars crashing, and a separate straining, snapping, twanging sound as the iron of the tower twisted.

The four massive concrete pylons that held the Eiffel Tower were ripping from the ground, lifting!

Down below, Paddy Nine Iron fell onto his back as the ground before him ripped open. Valin raced to grab onto the lowest handhold, but something, maybe

Paddy's helpless cry, turned him back.

He glared hatred up at Mack.

"You've grown strong, Mack!" Risky said in a snarl. "Now you will pay the price!"

She typed into her phone.

A text message that read, "Be the Destroyer!"

"If I hit Send, Mack, there will be no stopping the death and horror."

Mack noticed Stefan standing beside him, waiting, an expectant look on his face. He had no doubt what Stefan had in mind.

To both Risky and Stefan, Mack said, "Go for it."

Risky's face distorted into a lion's open mouth, filled with teeth. She roared her anger.

Stefan took three quick, running steps, leaped, and hit her feetfirst, very Jackie Chan.

Risky windmilled backward off the railing.

Mack ran to see, and she fell, facing upward, her hair a storm of red, laughing cruelly up at him. She held out the phone and he saw her thumb move.

Risky did not hit the ground. She had more tricks than that. Instead she slowed, and as she slowed she began to change shape.

Have you ever seen a sailboat suddenly flash out its sails all at once? It's very impressive. The wind will come up and the sailors will unfurl the sails and the wind will—*whoosh*—snap those sails open.

That's what Risky did with her vast, leathery wings. Which slowed her fall.

As did the long, barbed tail that stretched out from the base of her spine.

Her legs twisted forward, and toes became ripping, tearing talons.

Her arms were smaller, but there, too, fingers became talons.

She kept her eyes on Mack—malevolent, furious green eyes—but the rest of her face stretched forward, elongating into a long snout. A lizard's snout.

No.

"A dragon," Xiao said. "A western dragon!"

MEANWHILE . . .

"What's happening with you, Mack?" Camaro demanded.

The golem ran for the exit, desperate suddenly to get out of the school and away from the kids.

"I will become the Destroyer!" the golem cried, anguished.

"Hey!" Camaro said. "If anyone's becoming the destroyer, it's me!"

But Camaro had never seen what was coming now, never imagined it in her worst nightmare. The golem was changing. He was growing—not like he had when he was going to be a big boy, but taller, broader, more muscular, harder.

His five Mack fingers had melted into two on each hand. These were engorged, swelling, turning the color of dried blood.

Twin fangs, like the teeth of an ancient sabertoothed tiger, grew from his mouth, while twin upthrust tusks pushed through the sides of his mouth.

"Stop me!" the golem pleaded.

IN PARIS . . .

The leathery wings slowed Risky's fall, and with a little twist Risky turned over and swept easily around the tower at the height of the second floor.

Below, Paddy and Valin were pushing panicked

onlookers aside and forcing their way to the stairs.

But the Eiffel Tower continued to rip its way free of the earth.

Still in his loud voice, Mack cried, "The world is in danger! Everything you've seen on YouTube is true! Well . . . not everything. Just the stuff involving us!"

Risky took a long, slow turn out over the heads of the onlookers and came straight at the Magnifica.

"Beware!" Xiao cried. "She may be able to breathe fire!"

"True that!" Risky shouted gleefully. "And the first thing I fry is you, little annoying dragon person!"

"We need Vargran!" Jarrah cried.

"No!" Dietmar said. "We must stick to our plan!"

"We are going to move this tower!" Mack cried.

"Say what now?" the panicked onlookers cried in various accents of Gallic disbelief.

A jet of flame erupted from Risky's fanged mouth. But she was a little inexperienced when it came to breathing fire, and the blast of searing napalm shot by overhead. The flames were so intense that the gray-brown paint caught fire. The iron straps bent and twisted from the heat.

Risky swooped away, preparing to make another pass.

"We have to focus!" Jarrah cried. "All our power together!"

"She's coming back around!" Charlie yelled. "Man, I never thought I could hate a girl that pretty, but I think I've got it down now!"

"Here she comes!"

MEANWHILE . . .

"Stop me!" the golem pleaded.

And then Camaro spoke the words that were a sort of magic at Richard Gere Middle School.[38] The words were: "Bully emergency!"

She could yell when she wanted to, Camaro. Her voice carried. And throughout the school, all the bullies—the emo bully, the trendy bully, the goth bully, the nerd bully, the geek bully, and the rest—jumped from their seats and came at a run.

They pelted through slammed-open doors.

They leaped through windows (ground floor only).

They dropped whatever they were doing, and

---

38 I hardly think this is the time to . . . Oh, all right: Go, Fighting Pupfish!

whoever they were about to do it to, and came in a rush.

They saw then what the golem had become—a towering monster of mud with terrifying teeth and lobster claws and feet like a T. rex—and . . .

They ran away.

It's not that every bully is a coward; that would be overstating the case. It's just that they were much, much better at being tough to people who couldn't fight back. A nine-foot-tall killing machine was not really their specialty.

"Cowards!" Camaro roared at them.

She stood helpless, arms at her sides, muscles flexed, as the golem marched back to the school and stabbed his terrible lobster hands straight through the bricks of the science lab and emitted a heart-stopping bellow of rage and violence.

"Rrrraawwwrrrr!"

IN PARIS . . .

Risky aimed carefully this time. She came in slow, flaring her wings to keep her speed down.

"Fry, Magnifica, fry!" she said.

Flame—a wall of it—blew toward the Magnificent Seven (plus Stefan).

And just then, the Eiffel Tower tore free of the earth.

It was like a very badly maintained elevator. It shot up with such sudden acceleration that a dozen iron struts snapped and whirled like deadly whips in the air.

The flame went shooting past, beneath the airborne legs of the tower, which now rose, rose, slowing but still going up.

Some of the Parisians below allowed themselves a small sniff of surprise, and some even said, "*Mais c'est bizarre, ça.*" Which means, "That's a little odd."

Mack and his friends felt the sudden jolt of the freed tower in their legs. Their knees buckled, but they still held hands, they still kept alive the flow of *enlightened puissance.*

One way or the other, they had accomplished their goal of warning the world. Because one way or the other, they would be relocating the Eiffel Tower in a way that would be absolutely impossible to deny.

Ever.

By anyone.

And then all of it would become clear to the whole world. The Magnificent Twelve would be supported wherever they went.

If they lived that long.

The tower rose. It was impossible of course. The Eiffel Tower weighs 10,000 tons. A large car weighs less than two tons. So that's about 5,000 SUVs' worth of tower.

And yet . . . it rose!

Risky came around again, and this time she did not try a flying approach. She landed, head downward, on the upper third of the tower. Her talons grabbed the steels beams easily. The impact of her weight sent a shudder down to the feet of the Magnifica.

"This time I won't miss!" Risky said.

Foot over hand, she came down, closer and closer, as the tower rose higher. The Magnificent Seven held hands and kept their focus but now they were seconds from death and if they died the spell would break and the tower would fall. That would certainly make their point: that all of this was real, terribly real.

But it would also mean dropping more than a hundred stories of steel onto major thoroughfares, hotels and offices and apartments. The death toll would be disastrous.

"What do we do?" Rodrigo cried. His hand was firm, but the tall, aristocratic boy was sweating.

"Excellent question," Charlie said, snarky, but not running away, either.

So far, Mack was pleased with these two. He wouldn't mind getting to know them better.

Pity they all would be eight overcooked marshmallows at any moment.

Mack looked up and saw Risky, huge, glowering, liquid fire dribbling from her cruel reptilian mouth.

Xiao looked up, too, and said, "I am a dragon of China! If you threaten or harm me, you'll break the ancient treaty!"

"Yeah," Risky said sarcastically, her voice not at all changed by becoming a dragon. "That's a huge worry for me: your stupid little treaty."

"Maybe you should worry," Xiao said with amazing calm. "Maybe you should worry a lot."

Something about the confidence in her voice made Mack look around, like maybe there was a source of this almost absurd confidence.

And there was.

Three in fact.

They rose from behind the sparkling white dome of the church of Sacré-Coeur. They were like nothing that had been seen in the world since the earliest days of Paris, when it was only a handful of squalid thatched huts, a few bark fishing boats, filthy goats, and a small bistro.

Dragons!

"Did you call them?" Mack asked Xiao.

"No one calls a dragon, a dragon calls you," Xiao said. "They sense the presence of an interloper—a treaty breaker."

Risky had done a good job of turning herself into one of them. She was definitely quite dragonesque. But perhaps she had never seen the real thing, or at least didn't remember what they were like.

Because Risky was the dragon equivalent of, say, a machine gun. While the real ones, the ancient ones who had risen to defend their treaty, they were more like tanks.

Their wings were wider than city blocks.

As they flew, the downdraft alone was knocking cars and buses this way and that. Pedestrians were thrown against walls and down to the ground.

Just from the wind off their wings.

"Huh," Stefan said. It was an admiring "huh."

"Huh," Risky said. Hers was not an admiring

"huh." You can get a lot of different emotions across with just a "huh." And Risky's version was conveying some very real apprehension.

The dragons' speed was startling.

"You've broken the ancient treaty, Ereskigal," Xiao said. "They are required to punish you or risk war with the dragons of the east."

"Pfff," Risky said. "Nobody punishes me!"

She was brave. Give credit where it is due: she was brave. For another three seconds.

But there is just something about three massive, leathery, fire-breathing monsters the size of the largest bombers coming at you at eighty miles an hour that shakes your resolve.

"All right! All right!" Risky cried. Swiftly her scales and sinews, her talons and barbed tail, melted away to become her usual form again.

The dragons saw and swerved at the last minute. They blew past with such tornadic force that the tower itself spun twice before stabilizing.

Two of the dragons headed straight back in the direction of Sacré-Coeur, and Risky breathed a sigh of relief.

Standing on the railing again, she said, "Fine: I'll do it in a less dramatic fashion!"

She leveled her clenched fist at Mack. She spoke words that might have been Vargran, but might also have been some still more ancient—and more evil—language.

Mack stopped breathing. He wanted desperately to clutch his throat, but if he broke contact with the others . . .

And yet how long . . . face turning red . . . choking . . .

"Tough choice, eh, little Mack?" Risky taunted. "Hold on to the spell and die choking, or break it and die when the tower falls. Either one is good for me."

And that's when the third dragon swept by. Its wing tip grazed Risky. She wobbled. She cursed. She made a very angry, frustrated face.

And she fell backward into the air.

The tower was a hundred feet off the ground. Which meant the railing itself was about five hundred feet up in the air, round numbers.

Risky fell, but she glared hatred up at Mack. "The golem will kill everyone you loooooove!" she wailed.

And then, the dragon took aim and breathed a blast that was an inferno.

Risky's body burned, twisted, shriveled to something made out of charcoal dust, and then blew away on the breeze.

"She's dead!" Charlie exulted.

"Yeah, but not permanently," Jarrah said. "She'll be back."

The dragon returned and hovered in midair, obviously trying to avoid blowing them onto their backs. "Greetings, eastern cousin," it said in a strained, unnatural voice that sounded like a garbage truck lifting a Dumpster.

"Greetings, western cousin," Xiao said.

"This violation of the treaty was not our doing."

Xiao bowed her head slightly. "You seem to have rectified the situation."

The dragon . . . well, you wouldn't want to say he smiled because it was way too creepy to be a smile. In any case he said, "Rectified. Yes. Our eastern cousins are always good with words."

"Go in peace," Xiao said.

"For now," the dragon rumbled. Then he turned and swept back across the city, knocking down the people who had just gotten up.

"We must set this tower down," Sylvie said. "Let us place it in the Tuileries." When she saw blank looks, she said, "Over there, in the large garden beside the river."

Thus it came to pass that the Eiffel Tower, which had stood on the Left Bank of the Seine for more than a century, was relocated to the Right Bank.[39]

It's actually much more convenient.

And no one—not even conspiracy nuts—would be able to deny that something impossible, amazing, and absolutely magical had occurred.

The world would never be the same.

But at this particular moment, all of that meant very little to Mack.

With shaking fingers and his heart in his throat, he called the golem.

---

39 Don't go checking Google: they haven't updated yet.

Twenty-eight

MEANWHILE . . .

"**H**ey," Camaro said. "Don't be tearing up the school!"

To which the golem replied, "Gaaarrrrggh!"

"Seriously: if anyone is tearing up the school, it's going to be me," Camaro insisted.

The golem stabbed his second lobster claw right at her. She jumped nimbly aside, and the claw ripped up the ground where she had been standing.

"Hey!" she yelled.

The golem . . . well, the problem with the golem was that he wasn't what he had been anymore. He was no longer Mack. He was no longer even a silly fraud trying to pass himself off as Mack.

He was the Destroyer.

The golem jumped. It was a stunning thing to see, because he leaped in a single bound from the ground onto the top of the school building.

"Grraaawwwr!" he roared.

He stabbed his lobster claw down into the roof and threw aside bits of tile and plywood as if he was tearing into nothing more substantial than a cardboard box.

Camaro did the only thing she could think of. She took off one of her steel-studded wristbands and threw it at the golem. She had good aim. It hit him in the eye.

No, it didn't stop him. But it did distract him so that he put down the boy he had just snatched up through the roof.

His face dark with rage, the golem flew through the air and landed almost on top of Camaro. The impact knocked her down. She tried to get right back up, but the lobster claw stabbed the ground on either side of her, imprisoning her against the grass.

The golem lowered his face to within inches of hers.

He opened his mouth, baring terrible yellow teeth. He bellowed into her face, "GRRRooowwwwrRRR!" with such force it made her cheeks and lips shake.

"Hey! Stop!" Camaro yelled.

The teeth came closer.

"Stop or I will kick your butt!" Camaro raged.

The huge mouth opened. It encompassed Camaro's entire head. In a second that head would no longer be attached to her neck.

"Oh, man," she said. "And I really liked you."

The golem did not bite down. Instead its red-rimmed eyes blinked.

"Groowwwr?"

"Really," Camaro said to the inside of his mouth. "Look, maybe it's time I told you the truth. . . ."

Some people might say it was a little late for Camaro to be confessing anything, but you have to understand: she was not a trusting sort.

"Look, I always liked Mack and thought he was

cute. But I figured out a long time ago that you're not really Mack."

"Grrruuh?"

"You're sweeter than he is, for one thing. Not right now you're not, but usually."

The golem had now had her head inside his mouth and ready to bite for almost twenty seconds.

"I don't know what you are, maybe an alien or whatever, but I liked you. You know, before you became a ravening monster."

"Unnh," the golem said.

"Hey. Do you know there's a cell phone in here? In your mouth, I mean? Don't move."

He didn't move. He stayed perfectly still, crouched over her in a killing posture. With some difficulty, Camaro managed to stick her arm into his mouth. The phone was right there, just sitting beneath his forked tongue.

"Hey, you've got a text," she said. "'Be the Destroyer'?"

With even more awkwardness, she managed to extricate both her arm and the phone.

The golem pulled back then. It closed its huge

mouth but still crouched over the prone Camaro.

Camaro glared at the phone. "'Be the Destroyer'? Hey, no one pushes my boyfriend around except me." She hit the Reply button and typed in, "Drop dead!"

Now, here's the thing: there's never going to be any way to be sure about the exact timing. All we know is that at approximately the same time as Risky was falling, only to be incinerated midair by the dragon, Camaro hit Send.

Approximately the same time.

No one is saying for sure that the reason Risky wasn't able to nimbly escape the dragon is that Camaro had sent her a fatal text on an enchanted phone.

But it would absolutely serve Risky right.

Camaro sat up, wiped away some monster saliva, and took a long, hard look at the creature before her. He was no longer the Destroyer. He also wasn't Mack.

He was a muddy-looking creature with only the barest of features. He looked like something a child would fashion out of dirt and twigs.

"So. What are you exactly?" Camaro asked.

"I am . . . I am a golem. I am whatever I have been told to be. First I was told to 'be Mack.' Then I was told to 'be the Destroyer.'"

He shrugged, obviously a little embarrassed. (Understandable, really, since the entire student body of Richard Gere Middle School[40] was fleeing out of the other side of the somewhat damaged building.)

"You're covering for Mack, huh?" she asked.

"That's what I was made to do."

Camaro thought about that. And she sighed. "Well, like I said, I like Mack. So keep covering for him. But, dude: be yourself."

"I . . . I don't know what myself is like."

She nodded as though this was wise. And it kind of was. "All right then, be Mack. But when you're done being Mack, hang out with me; I'll get you straightened out."

Of course she ended up having to write that down. Because it doesn't matter if it's a tiny paper scroll or a text message: if you want to get a golem to do something, you have to put it in writing.

On a small scrap of paper Camaro wrote, "Be Mack. Also my friend."

Just then the golem's other phone—the nonmagical one—rang. Camaro answered it. The golem was busy returning to his Mack-like appearance.

40 Go, Fighting Pupfish! Why not?

"T'sup, MacAvoy?" Camaro said.

She enjoyed the long silence on the other end.

"Um . . . ," he said at last.

"Don't worry. I got this," Camaro said, and hung up the phone.

Last Chapter Before the Next Book

Headlines from the next day's websites and newspapers:

New York Times:
EIFFEL TOWER RELOCATION:
ARCHITECTURE CRITICS WEIGH IN

Le Monde:
TOURISTE AMERICAIN VOLE TOUR EIFFEL

Fox News:
ERESKIGAL WOULD RAISE
TAXES ON JOB CREATORS

High Times:
NO WAY! WAY? NO WAY!

Deadline Hollywood:
ONE PERCENTERS ON TRAIL OF MACK RIGHTS

Huffington Post:
PALE QUEEN SEEN AT REPUBLICAN RALLY

Wall Street Journal:
EXCHANGES OPEN LOWER ON APOCALYPSE FEARS

The Sun:
FROGS IN AWFUL EIFFEL MIX-UP

The clearest of the many YouTube videos had 17,903,022 hits. Most commenters believed it had been faked.

An exhausted Mack was in the very posh bathroom of a very nice room in a very nice Paris hotel. The police had decided against arresting him and his friends—for now. But they were definitely not supposed to leave the city.

Mack wasn't too worried about that. He and the others had just flown the Eiffel Tower across Paris: they could deal with some cops.

He took a shower, toweled off, and got dressed.

Then he caught a reflection in the chrome pipe at the back of the toilet.

He sighed.

"Where have you been?" he said, and crouched down to better see the wavy, uncertain image there.

Grimluk—looking as grim as ever—said, "My time is shoooooort, Mack. I am weak . . . I fade. . . ."

"Yeah, well, you know what? I feel the same exact way, dude."

"Bad day?"

"Yes. Very bad." But then he grinned. "On the other hand, we have seven of us now. And the whole world has been warned about what's coming."

"The whole world? But that would take many messengers, riding for months to the far corners of the earth to spread the word. To far-off Azkebal and frigid Gramaton, and steaming Bakersfield and—"

"Also, we have the Key," Mack said, interrupting what sounded like a list that might go on for quite some time.

Grimluk blinked as Mack pulled the two parts of the Key from his backpack hanging on the door. "See? Also, the Loch Ness monster is a duck now . . . long story."

"Very well done, Mack of the Magnifica."

It occurred to Mack that it was the first compliment he'd ever gotten from Grimluk.

"Now what?" Mack asked, not sure he wanted to hear the answer.

"Now, Mack, you must find your own roots. You must learn the truth of your own distant past. For only then will you understand Valin's treachery, and only then can you hope to assemble . . . the . . ."

And then Grimluk disappeared.

Mack sat down backward on the toilet and waited. In a few seconds Grimluk faded back in.

". . . let me go to my final rest," the ancient, gnarled, wrinkled, dusty, green-toothed, hunched, milky-eyed old apparition said.

"What was that?" Mack asked, frowning.

". . . past is in far Punjab . . . bury me . . ."

"Whoa, whoa, whoa there, Grimluk. Hey, what's this about burying you? You're supposed to be running this whole thing!"

Grimluk almost smiled, which was close enough given the state of his oral hygiene. No one wanted a better look at those choppers.

"It is foretold: before the Pale Queen rises, the last of . . . must die."

"You are in and out, try again!" Mack urged, gripping the pipe.

"I fade . . . weak . . ."

"Hey! Hey!"

But Grimluk did not reappear.

Mack finally gave up and went into the living room, where the others were eating a breakfast of croissants, brioches, jam, and hot chocolate.

"You look as if you have seen a ghost," Sylvie said.

"Let's hope not," Mack said. He took an empty seat and poured himself a cup of hot chocolate. "So, does anyone know if there really is a place called Punjab?"

Opa-ma eb twif!

Turn the page for a sneak peek
at Mack's continuing adventures in
The Magnificent 12: The Power.

BOOK FOUR

THE POWER

Not Far from the Earth's Molten Core (Present Day)

Princess Ereskigal, whose friends (she had no friends) all called her Risky, was having a very difficult conversation with her mother, the Pale Queen.

"Are they destroyed?" the Pale Queen nagged. "Are the new Magnificent Twelve all dead?"

The Pale Queen could appear in just about any form she chose, but for the purposes of this particular conversation she was wearing one of her favorite forms:

as tall as a moderate redwood tree, with a gigantic head—a quite beautiful head in some ways, but with skin so translucent that in the right light you could see the bones of her skull and her jaw and the individual teeth in her head, thirty-six of them in all, each long and sharp and curved back to facilitate the swallowing of large, whole, usually living things.

Her hair was white. Actually it was colorless if you looked at an individual strand, but taken all together it was white (like a polar bear). It went down to her bony shoulders, from which hung a floor-length robe made out of screams.

Not the sort of outfit you find for sale at your local mall. But the Pale Queen wove reality out of fear and loss and despair.

The dress had a cutaway so that you could see her powerful calves filling boots as tall as city light posts. The boots were dragon skin and used human skulls to make a row of buckles. The toes of the boots were about as big as canoes—sharp, barbed-steel canoes.

Frankly, Risky thought, the outfit was a bit "young" for her mother. But she wasn't going to say anything about it unless her mother really annoyed her. She was holding that in reserve.

"Mother, I said I would do it, didn't I?" Risky huffed.

"So, the new Magnificent Twelve have been destroyed?"

"Are you saying you don't trust me?" Risky crossed her arms over her chest and actually stamped her foot.

Like the Pale Queen, Risky could take any form. But generally she preferred to appear as an extraordinarily attractive teenage girl with luscious red hair and eyes so green there was no way they could possibly be entirely human.

Her dress was a simple, formfitting thing with a neckline that was daring without being "too much." And she most often went barefoot.

"I trust . . . NO ONE!" the Pale Queen raged. And when she raged, her minions—Skirrit, Tong Elves, Gudridan, Lepercons, and so on—were blown back like action figures in the blast of a leaf blower.

Risky wasn't blown anywhere.

She feared her mother, as any sensible daughter would. There wasn't a lot of motherly love in this family, and the Pale Queen could absolutely decide to gobble her daughter up like a shrimp. Which was exactly what she had done to Risky's father.

Like a shrimp.

But at the same time, the Pale Queen needed Risky. For another few days the Pale Queen was bound by a powerful spell and could not escape the World Beneath and go romping around up top where all the tasty humans lived.

Risky, however, could.

Which meant Risky could take on jobs like eliminating the terrible threat posed by the Magnificent Twelve. A task she had so far failed to accomplish despite several attempts.

"I don't think you're taking this seriously," the Pale Queen said more quietly, her tone larded with guilt-inducing disappointment.

"I am so," Risky countered.

"No, you're not."

"Uh-huh!"

"No."

"Yah-ha-ah!"

"I just don't want you being distracted. Remember the last time?"

That was unfair.

That was a cheap shot.

A low blow.

Because yes, Risky did remember the last time she'd made a promise to her mother, a thousand years ago. . . .

. . . And as you can see by the ellipses, the three little dots there, we're going to tell that story. Later. But first, on to chapter 1.

One

It turned out the Punjab was in India. Did you know that? No, you didn't; don't pretend. But don't feel bad, either, because David "Mack" MacAvoy also had no idea where the Punjab was until very recently. He's learned a lot about the Punjab lately.

For instance, he learned that the Punjab is a warm, sunny place, at least at this particular time of year. Mack noticed how sunny and warm it was because he was on the ground staring right up at that warm sunny sun.

He was on the ground because creatures called Brembles were keeping him there.

Do you know what a Bremble is? Probably not, because Brembles no longer exist. (The last Bremble died in 1797, and he was quite old by then.) Brembles were a hybrid species, not something that occurred naturally, but a species created by evil forces. Imagine a large gorilla. No, twice that big. Now imagine that instead of being a peaceable plant eater, that oversized gorilla was extremely unpleasant. Now imagine that instead of fur, that extremely unpleasant oversized gorilla was covered in something very like porcupine quills. So, already: not good.

But now imagine that the porcupine quills were the least of it, because where a gorilla would have hands, Brembles had what looked like some terrible explosion of thorns, spikes, and razor wire. From the center of this melee of thorns, spikes, and razor wire protruded one spike, longer than the others, which was known as a chulk. This chulk was split so that it was really two spikes with a narrow gap between them, rather like two tines of a fork.

It was these chulks that the Brembles used to pin

7

Mack in place. They had driven their chulks deep into the ground in such a way as to pin his four limbs down.

In addition to being staked out, he was also stretched a bit so that the muscles in his chest felt almost as if they might tear. This made it hard to breathe, which in turn made it hard to scream, which was okay because there was no one to come to his rescue.

Did he want to scream? Definitely.

Mack was utterly unable to reach a hand to his face, which was a shame because there were red ants crawling into his ears and nose and scouting around his eyeballs. These were not the little ants you might see at a picnic. These ants were not trying to get at the coleslaw. Unless coleslaw is a euphemism for Mack's brain.

Mack had a pretty good view of one ant in particular that was walking right across his eyeball—his left eyeball, as it happened. Mack blinked furiously, hoping to discourage the ant, but each sweep of his eyelid just knocked the ant around a little, which is no way to discourage an ant.

Seen in extreme close-up, the ant was like some fuzzy, out-of-focus, terrifying alien robot. It had six legs, a carapace, and a rounded-off pyramid of a head with huge, elongated pincers on the front. It had little black BBs for eyes. And its tail had a stinger like a combination claw and shot needle that would squirt painful venom if stabbed into something.

Like, say, an eyeball.

In all honesty, the ants were not as creepy as the giraffe-necked beetles that had been exploring Mack's face just minutes before. But Mack had gotten rid of the beetles using his enlightened puissance—the mystical power possessed by only a few—and some words from the Vargran language—known to even fewer.

All he'd had to do was yell, "Lom-ma fabfor!" and the beetles had disappeared. Mack had been studying his Vargran. He was all Vargraned up. He had come to the Punjab ready for trouble. Just one little problem: the enlightened puissance isn't some endless water faucet with power just flowing out like, well, water. No, it's more like a drip drip drip of water. It comes, then it stops, then slowly, sloooowly it builds back up until there's enough to drip. A treasonous Tong Elf had once told him it took a full day, but Tong Elves lied. Still, it took a while, and while you were waiting for it to build back up . . . you'd find that ants had replaced the beetles, and now where were you?

Well, you were staked out by the chulks of Brembles in the Punjab with ants in your eyeballs, that's where you were.

"Ahhhh!" he gasped because right then an ant bit him. Not the eyeball ant. An ear ant. An ant just inside his ear. The bottom part of the ear canal, if you want to be really specific.

It felt exactly like someone had heated a needle over a fire and then stabbed it into his ear canal. Not good.

"Ahhhh!" Mack cried again, straining for breath. "That hurts!"

"Aha! I see they are biting," Valin gloated. "That's very bad news, Mack, my timeless foe, because once one ant starts, they all get into it. Within a minute, a hundred ants will sink their painful stingers into you! You will cry out in pain. Then you will swell up. And of course: die. And thus will my family's honor be avenged!"

"I am not your timeless foe, you lunatic!"

Valin was standing over him but providing no shade from the blazing sun above. He was dressed flamboyantly in puffy zebra-striped pantaloons, black leather boots that rose to his knees, and a purple vest over no shirt. To top it all off, he had an amazing hat that looked like the kind of thing Puss in Boots or maybe a pirate might wear. It had an actual pink feather. From his wide belt hung a dagger and a short sword.

It was an eccentric look.

Beyond Valin stood the terrible Nafia assassin Paddy "Nine Iron" Trout. Paddy was an elderly gentleman dressed all in green. Green suede shoes, green slacks, a green-and-yellow waistcoat over a very pale green shirt but beneath a bright-green sport coat. And to top it off there was a green bowler hat.

Even in India, which is a diverse and tolerant country known for interesting clothing, Valin and Paddy stood out. It's not every day you see a pantalooned twelve-year-old with a sword traveling with a green-clad hundred-year-old Nafia assassin.

"Just let me kill . . . ," Paddy wheezed. He stopped, pulled a clear plastic respirator mask from his inside coat pocket, put it over his mouth and nose, and drew a deep breath. Then another.

And . . . another.

And . . .

. . . one more.

"Him," Paddy said finally, concluding the sentence which had begun, "Just let me kill."

Valin shook his head. "You are my mentor, Nine Iron, but this is a matter of family honor. First he must endure a hundred fiery stings!"

"As you . . . ," Paddy began.

And . . . breathed.

Okay, one more . . .

"Wish," Paddy concluded.

"Let me go!" Mack cried. He pulled at the chulks, but no, he wasn't pulling his way out of this one. The Brembles had him. Valin had him.

And the ants had him.

A second ant stung.

A third.

And now the stinging signal went out through all the ants.

Mack was about to die a most terrible death.

Really.